I could feel Porter's green eyes on me as I crossed the parking lot, my sharp heels stabbing into the soft tar that had spent the day in the sun.

My face flushed and my pace quickened as I realized that at this moment I was not jealous of Yorke, not at all. Not of her engagement, or huge diamond ring, and especially not of Roger, a whose shoes and belt matched the interior of his car.

I reached the stairs and paused, burning a memory in my mind, one that was all mine, that didn't involve my sisters.

His eyes, the green so bright, the sideways smile, the way it felt when he held my hand. My fingers tingled still, and I wrapped them into a fist, trying to hold on tight.

"Hurry up," my sisters called out to me from the entrance, and I followed after them, one step behind. It was Yorke, Freddie, and then me, like always, up the curved stairs and into the club.

CHRISTINA MEREDITH

Kiss
Crush
Collide

Greenwillow Books

An Imprint of HarperCollins *Publishers*

Kiss Crush Collide
Copyright © 2012 by Christina Meredith

The text of this book is set in ITC Novarese. Book design by Sylvie Le Floc'h.

Library of Congress Cataloging-in-Publication Data

Meredith, Christina.
Kiss crush collide / by Christina Meredith.
p. cm.
"Greenwillow Books."
Summary: Leah's path has been laid out for her by her controlling mother and perfect sisters—prom queen, valedictorian, college, country club wedding—but when Leah meets a boy who is not in her social class, she begins to question what she wants for herself.
ISBN 978-0-06-206224-6 (trade bdg.)—ISBN 978-0-06-206225-3 (pbk.)
[1. Social classes—Fiction. 2. Self-realization—Fiction. 3. Sisters—Fiction. 4. Family problems—Fiction.] I. Title.
PZ7.M534Co 2012   [Fic]—dc22   2011002838

12 13 14 15 16 CG/RRDH 10 9 8 7 6 5 4 3 2 1
First paperback edition, 2013.

 Greenwillow Books

For my Freddie
and my Yorke

One

"**L**eah!" My mother rolls her eyes, sounding completely exasperated as she steps down the three thick stone slabs at our front door, her heels clacking. Leaving the double doors flung open behind her, she bends down and examines one of the yellow rosebushes that line every inch of our driveway.

Shane slowly rolls the convertible alongside her, and we grind to a stop on the thick carpet of gravel, just behind a small red M3 I don't recognize. Shane pulls up the emergency brake with a crank, and my mother stands, smoothing the hem of her sweater, wilted yellow petals drifting to her feet. "Thank God you're finally home."

"You know I have practice till four," I say. Her heels sink into the sea of salt-and-pepper pebbles with a crunch, the bright metallic sound of the three thin silver bracelets she never takes off trailing behind her as she walks out into the middle of our circular drive.

"We were starting to get worried," she says, raising her eyebrows at me, ignoring my scowl. The bracelets slip down her arm one by one, *shink, shink, shink,* as she reaches up and gives my boyfriend her standard greeting, a kiss on the left cheek that leaves a coral stain.

"Just like always," I mumble to myself, and lean over, pushing the heavy car door open with a huff. I feel the part of my butt cheek that has become one with the sun-baked seat peel away as I climb out of the car. I kick the door shut behind me with my heel before Shane can even manage to untangle himself from my mother and jog his way around the front of the car to help me out.

"Oh, Shane." My mother's laughter bubbles up, floating over the sound of his size twelves chewing up the gravel, trying to catch up with me. "You're too good to her. You know she's kept us all waiting."

I stop. Her bracelets brush together again with a silvery sound as my mother and my boyfriend step past me. She walks him up the front stairs and into the house, her heels echoing across the canyon of black-and-white tile we call a foyer. I unclench my hand just long enough to push the button on the side of my phone to check the time. It's 4:12.

Standing on the curb in front of the school's entrance exactly eight minutes earlier, I cocked my head and twisted my hair, cursing Shane under my breath.

"Come on, come on, come on," I breathed, my unwillingness to drive factoring into my frustration, ratcheting it up a notch, as I bounced impatiently in the tiny square of shade cast by a yellow school zone sign, while I watched the entire student body roll by in front of me, free for the day.

It's not that I can't drive. I just don't. Shane asked me out the second day of our sophomore year. I slid into the passenger seat on our first date. Shane climbed behind the wheel, smiled, crooked two fingers around the curve of the wheel, and dropped his other hand onto my left knee. It's almost two years later, and not much has changed.

I got a car, just like my sisters did—it's a sweet sixteen standard—but mine just seems to sit in our driveway. It's cute and fun, a shiny bright blue convertible bug, and I think it's in the exact same spot it was when my dad handed over the keys, hugged me tight, and wished me a happy birthday.

Sometimes he threatens to drive it himself when he goes to the golf course, and I try to picture his fuzzy covered clubs sticking out of the tiny backseat, but he always ends up backing out the company truck instead, JOHNSON CUSTOM CONSTRUCTION—WE BUILD BIG HOUSES, sliding past the kitchen window as he drives off in the early-morning light.

My parents have been together forever, high school sweethearts destined for domestic bliss. My dad started his construction business right after school, building a tiny house for the two of them. Over the years the business got bigger, the houses got bigger, and his truck got huge.

It's so big now that it beeps when it backs up, driving my mother crazy if she hasn't had her morning latte yet. She yaps around the kitchen like a little dog until he shifts into drive and rolls away.

I don't know why my parents don't get rid of my car. I wouldn't mind. But my mother says of course I'll want a car when I go off to college. My oldest sister, Yorke, drives her car everywhere on campus. I can picture her, all ballsy and blond, double-parking her BMW in front of every lecture hall, carelessly dropping cardboard boxes onto her leather seats when she makes beer runs for her sorority sisters, pissing off the campus cops on a daily basis. I am sure my dad has the tickets to prove it.

My cell said 4:04. Which meant that I had gotten out of practice, collected all my stuff, and jogged out here in less than four minutes. It's Friday, and that means yet another Friday night family dinner at the club. It's a tradition my mother instituted when we were little, back in the days when she could dress us up in matching pastel dresses.

Tonight we will be celebrating my sister Freddie's valedictorianness. Freddie is less brassy than Yorke, in color and volume. She is perfection. Her big graduation party with the tent and the band and the whole world invited is tomorrow. Tonight is just for family, and I can't be late.

Not that I can ever be late, really, with my mother running the show, but especially not tonight. I'm sure she was expecting me at least four minutes ago. She seems to think that Shane drives a time machine, not a convertible Mercedes.

I looked up from my phone and saw Dani and Len waving to me from the parking lot, red and gold poms stuffed under their arms, purses and bags slung everywhere. I smiled and waved back.

Valerie Dickens, math genius and serious contender for future senior class valedictorian, was slinking along the hot pavement, lurking a few steps behind my two best friends. Valerie and I used to be close. Until the fourth grade, when the geography of our new house and her serious competitive streak separated us.

Thin, spindly, and slightly translucent, she slid around the cars like something you would poke at in the bottom of a petri dish. She looked over at me with a scowl.

I dropped my hand so fast when her eyes met mine that my bag slid off my shoulder with a jerk and practically yanked my hair from my head.

She stuck a key into the door of a dark green VW, an oversize rusty cheese grater with bald tires and a bad dent in the back end. I watched her pry the door open. The stack of books that had been cradled in her arms slipped and spread out across the sticky blacktop, spines cracking. I didn't have to watch her stoop to pick them up, I knew what they were: *Trigonometry*, *Applied Mathematics*, and *The Catcher in the Rye*. She stood, frizzy hair hanging in her face, and gave me the same knowing look she had given me only an hour before.

The final bell had just rung, waking up half the class, when Mr. Hobart stopped by my desk and said, "Johnson, hang back for a second. I have a matter to discuss with you."

It is not a treat to have AP Calc as the last class of the day. And toward the end of the semester even the thought of the class has been leaving me with a burning knot in my stomach.

I used to not even think about AP Calc. It used to be like most of my classes—easy, doable, not a lot of effort. Then somewhere during these last few weeks we took a quantum leap and entered a world that makes absolutely no sense to me. Zero.

I have been getting by with a lot of guessing and by copping Freddie's old notes and papers. She keeps *everything*, every bit of schoolwork, every scrap of paper, anything she ever did since kindergarten. It's kind of sad.

My grades must finally be slipping or why else would Mr. Hobart want to talk to me? Fighting the urge to curl up like a shrimp and rock back and forth at my desk, I got up, grabbed my bag and my books, and walked toward the front of the room, thinking, Say good-bye to ever being valedictorian.

Mr. Hobart has a huge metal table parked at the front of his classroom that he uses as a command station. With stacks and stacks of papers, probably dating back to the 1970s, his organizational system is legendary. He can reach blindly into a pile while lecturing and extract exactly the right paper.

I was tempted to throw the windows open wide and watch the papers and his toupee flutter back down to earth. Instead I mentally prepared a speech about my trying harder and his being a great teacher and how much I have learned, and then I planned on finishing it all off with a big smile.

"So, Little Johnson," Mr. Hobart said, his stubby, ink-covered fingers tapping along the edge of his tin table like he was sending a telegram. I smiled at him and his stacks of papers placed at right angles and remembered the first time I had heard someone call me that.

It happened the first week that all three of us,

Yorke, Freddie, and I, were in high school at the same time. I had just shown up for freshman gym class, all short shorts and ponytail and fresh summer tan, when I heard some older boys up in the balcony. They were leaning over the railing, watching the freshman girls file into the gym.

"Look, it's Little Johnson," one of them said in a deep voice.

I glanced up, and some random guy I'm pretty sure I'd seen Yorke kissing in our driveway late one night pointed at me.

"Hey, Little Johnson," he called out, and I looked around the room before I looked up at him again, very aware of myself standing outside the circle of girls on the shining, wooden floor.

Some other guy with big, meaty arms laughed and said, "I like me some Little Johnson."

I was flattered and embarrassed and confused all at the same time. And suddenly very conscious of my exposed legs and how tight my T-shirt was.

Finally, Ms. Kemp blew her whistle and shouted, "Line up, girls!"

She called out our names, and we lined up, matching shorts and Ts all in a row.

When Ms. K got to me, she glanced up from her clipboard, smirked, and yelled, "Little Johnson!"

With a very Yorke-like curtsy, I took my place at the front of the third line amid low whistles and laughter from the balcony above. The name has been with me ever since. I just wish it didn't make me sound like a tiny dick.

Mr. Hobart finally found the paper he was looking for and handed it to me. "Your ability to show your work really helped boost your grade," he said.

I slowly reached for the paper. I recognized my deliberate, detailed work. It was my AP Calc final with a large A minus written in the upper right corner. I guess I had been holding my breath because when I finally breathed, it came out in a whoosh that disturbed the closest stack but not Mr. Hobart's hair. He pinned the papers down with a thick thumb. I was a bit stunned.

"An A minus?" I asked. I was hoping for a C. To be honest, a C minus really seemed more likely when

I remembered how much looking out the window and hair twisting I had done during the exam. I held the paper out toward Mr. Hobart, ready for it to be returned to its resting place at the bottom of a pile. It didn't seem mine to keep.

He took the exam from me, lifted a year's worth of papers like a magician splits a deck of cards, and inserted my paper deftly somewhere in the middle. I'll bet he could find it again, even after a shuffle, with a blindfold on.

He stood and looked me straight in the eyes through his thick black-rimmed glasses.

"Your sister Freddie struggled a bit too during the last semester of my class," he said.

He put his hand at the small of my back and spoke quietly, leading me toward the classroom door. "Consider it a sneak peak, if you will. Go off and enjoy your summer, Leah. Rest assured that our hopes for a third Johnson valedictorian are intact."

He stopped abruptly. Valerie Dickens was milling about in the open doorway, her arms laden down with textbooks, her expression unsettled, obviously having heard everything. Mr. Hobart waved me out the door, and I slipped past Valerie without meeting her eyes.

I headed toward the gym for my last practice of the year. I am sure Valerie had studied her ass off for that test. In fact I am sure she had studied her ass off all semester. I recognized that look on her face. I've seen it before, at dances, tryouts, parties, in the girls' bathrooms, school hallways, and classrooms, all my life actually.

My mother and sisters say it is just jealousy, but I have the feeling there is more to it than that. I get that girls like Valerie might want something to hate about me—herpes, dandruff, even the occasional breakout—because mostly my life happens while I smile and watch. But they put in the time. They aim for the prize, stay home on Friday nights to study, get up early on school days to practice. They read and memorize and put their hearts into it and ache for boys who pay no attention. I just show up and get everything they're after. I would probably hate me, too.

But summer is almost here. Graduating seniors were done today; the rest of us have three long days of exams, results, and hot, closed classrooms still to go. I heaved a sigh and cracked open the tall metal gym door for my last pep squad practice of the year.

A loud, pounding dance beat and the stale smell of sweat hit me along with the realization that Valerie was going to spend the summer waiting and wondering about her class standing, but being third in such a fine line of sisters, I was all set. I had three whole months of sunny absolution spread out in front of me. So I did what any good Johnson would do; I smoothed down my shirt, shook out my hair, and bounced out onto the gym floor with a big smile.

The smell of patchouli hits me before I can even make it to the top of the stairs.

"Freddie must be practicing for her year abroad," I whisper to Shane over my shoulder, stopping to fan my hand in front of my face.

Our bodies bounce into each other as I lag and Shane advances. Prodding me from behind, pressing solid and strong, he's urging me toward the top of the stairs and the possibility that he is going to get some as soon as we get to my room.

"If you're lucky she is growing her armpit hair out, too," I say, delaying the inevitable with my arms out, weight suspended from the polished banisters, knowing that Shane thinks Freddie is hot. Everybody does. She is.

He smiles back at me, all white teeth and good manners, unwilling to comment and risk the possibility of pissing off one of my sisters. Shaking his head, he wrinkles up his straight, slightly sunburned nose and slides his fingers tightly around mine as we trip up the last carpeted step.

"I heard that," Freddie yells as soon as we turn into the hall. "And you're late."

I drop Shane's hand and step into Freddie's doorway. Sniffing, I can just make out a top note of nail polish swirling above the cloud of patchouli. Freddie is on her unmade bed, curled over her toes, an open bottle of fruit punch-colored polish on the small shawl-covered table next to her.

It seems like everything in Freddie's room is recently shawl covered. Or scarf covered. The lamps all burn faintly under fringed scarves. The chairs, dressing table, desk, bookshelves, even the bed— all draped.

She is getting a jump start on her foreign exchange experience. Next year she will be living in France, and this year I guess we all are. The sounds, compliments of an almost endless loop of conversational French playing through her iPod speakers, with an occasional bout of Edith Piaf, the sights, even the scent of Paris spill from Freddie's room 24-7. J'aime Paris and all that, but I don't know if I will make it to next fall.

"I got here in twelve minutes," I say flatly, leaning against Freddie's door frame, twisting my hair around my fingers in frustration. Twelve, I think, mentally navigating the maze of hallways, stop signs, and ass grabbing I had to navigate with Shane in that short period of time.

"Just how fast does she want Shane to drive?" I ask.

Freddie stops painting and leans back against the crazy pile of orange, pink, red, and purple pillows that threatens to take over her bed. She waves her hands around over her feet, homecoming queen style, in what can only be an attempt to speed up the drying process. I have a miniflashback, leaning there at the edge of Freddie's stinky pink room, to last fall, when she was perched up on the back of a convertible wearing a sparkly green dress and a silver crown, shivering in the sharp air as she rolled by in the homecoming parade, waving those same cupped, stiff hands at me and the crowd.

"Faster," she says while testing a nail for stickiness. She looks up at me and adds, unnecessarily, "Obviously."

"It's not like I missed anything," I say, dismissing the total duh face she is making at me from her bed. Staring down, I snap off some of the hair that is woven around my fingers like golden thread, feeling each strand stretch before it breaks with a sudden little pop. Shane reaches for me, pulling at my hand. I let his warm fingers slip through mine.

"That's what you think," Freddie says almost sagely, her expression unreadable behind a curtain of long blond hair as she picks up the bright little brush, starts fresh on her pinkie toe, and I wonder what she means.

Shane tries his luck again, pulling more impatiently this time, and I give in, letting him lure me away from Freddie and Edith and whatever it is that I may have missed. Hooking my fingers around his, I drag my toes through the thick cream carpet all the way down the hall, feeling his pull getting stronger and stronger the closer we get to my door. He knows my mother's nerves may have been momentarily settled now that I am home safe, but the sound of her uptight heels clicking across the tiled foyer downstairs means we are running out of time.

Two

Roger has perfectly trimmed dark hair that stands up in a neat line along the edge of his forehead, like a hedge. He also has sharp creases down the front of his khakis and fine, shiny driving moccasins that match his leather belt. His arms are tan from golfing; his face is tan from skiing in the winter and from summers manning the barbecue at his family's lake house. So, in short, he is just like every boyfriend Yorke has ever had, but with maybe a little bit more money, as I discovered that evening while waiting with my sisters on our front steps for a ride to the club and he pulled up in the little red M3 Shane and I had parked behind earlier that day.

This manicured man is now standing with an arm wrapped tightly around my oldest sister's waist as the soft tinkling notes from the club's piano bar drift over to our table. Our middle school music teacher is moonlighting for tips. Hunching over the gleaming black baby grand in the corner, her frizzy hair bounces in time as her eyes, magnified to the tenth power by her thick, smudged glasses, trail along on the photocopied sheet music. She pauses a moment for applause at the end of each piece, then silently cracks her knuckles and starts in on another melancholy, boozy tune.

My dad sits at the head of the table, his smile beaming out into the room. My mother, to his right, dabs at her eyes, leaving dark mascara spots across her expensive linen country club napkin.

I look around the table, my wineglass at half-mast. We are supposed to be celebrating Freddie's graduation, yet only Shane and Evan, Freddie's boyfriend whom she is planning to dump at the end of the summer so she can get buck wild during her year abroad, seemed truly surprised to hear Yorke's engagement news. They jumped up and clapped, giving themselves away as outsiders. The rest of us were already in on it.

Yorke could never keep a secret. Ever. She was always the one who guessed where our Christmas gifts were hidden each year. Then she would convince me, or Freddie, but usually me since Freddie kind of has an iron will, to come along on the expedition to uncover them.

If we refused, Yorke would find the gifts herself and then, afterward, pin us down and tell us what we were getting. I remember being under the stairs in my dad's office late one December afternoon when I was about eight, holding a big yellow flashlight while Yorke shifted boxes around and called out everything she found. "Dollhouse . . . board game . . . dresses . . . books for Freddie . . . paint set." My heart dropped and the flashlight bobbed every time she found another box.

For other occasions, she would tell you what a

present was just as you were starting to tear off the wrapping paper. It was like someone snuffing out the candles on your cake just as you were about to blow, your lungs full of air and your mind full of wishes and then whoosh . . . gone.

It didn't matter whom the gift was from or whom it was for; she had to tell. And not just us. I remember going to birthday parties as kids. Yorke got us invited to everything, as she is, and was even then, the most popular and social person I have ever met.

We would walk in the front door, wearing our matching but different-colored dresses, and Yorke would hand over our perfectly wrapped gift and announce baldly, "It's a baby doll." Then she would walk away to pin the tail on the donkey or join the circle of little girls with freshly brushed hair and pink dresses who were just dying to play with her and Freddie and I would be left standing, embarrassed, in the front hall with an upset mother and a confused little birthday girl.

She didn't grow out of it.

"Leah, you made the squad!" she screamed just

thirty minutes after I had finished my freshman pep squad tryout. We weren't supposed to know the results until the next morning, so did I mind keeping it a secret until then? "Leah, I heard you got captain!" she cheered, calling from her dorm room the next year, an insider even when she was on the outside. She knew before I did, before anyone else did, and of course she had to be the first to tell. It was the same thing with her engagement; she even had to trump herself.

We had been driving along in Roger's red convertible earlier that night, the smooth tan leather seats smelling new and expensive, his frat boy rock barely loud enough to be heard over the sizzle of the tires and the swirl of the warm June breeze. Freddie and I were squeezed in the back, our short black dresses fluttering, our legs angled toward the middle, knees knocking together, as we pulled out of our driveway for the short trip to the country club. Yorke lowered the volume on the power ballad as soon as we hit the street and turned around to face us.

"Guess what?" she gushed, and I leaned forward, gripping the side of her seat with my fingers. Roger gunned it just as she squealed, "Roger and I are engaged!" and she was snapped back into her seat, momentarily pinned down by the force of the engine.

I took this opportunity to look to my right at Freddie, who was sitting back in her seat, her eyebrows raised. She smiled at me and then turned her head to look at the passing countryside. I settled back. Of course she already knew. Freddie and Yorke are alike in a lot of ways, but not this one. Freddie can keep a secret. She's like a vault.

Yorke swiveled back around, and I plastered a huge grin on my face as Roger jerked us into a higher gear.

"I was going to wait until we made the big announcement tonight at dinner, but I just couldn't . . . " she said as she smoothed her hair back with her right hand, pausing long enough for me to see the weighty diamond sparkling on her finger. "Don't say anything to Mother or Dad, okay? I mean, they already know, but still, act surprised, okay?"

"Okay." I nodded, going along with Yorke's scheme, like always. "Now," I said with a big breath, "let me see that ring."

Yorke held out her hand just as Roger took a wild right, the swing of the car pulling her fingers away from mine. I grabbed on to Yorke's seat and steadied myself. I looked up to see Roger smiling benignly at me in the rearview mirror.

It seemed a bit dangerous to be crowded up near the front of the car with Yorke's diamond, Freddie's knees, and Roger's testosterone, so I leaned back and listened to Yorke's stream of wedding plans: cream roses, champagne cocktails, and strawberry dresses. Or maybe that was cream-colored dresses and strawberry champagne cocktails?

I looked out over the lake as we whizzed by. It was smooth, the water dark with splashes of sunlight trailing a boat or two. There were dads and kids out on the docks, tying up Sunfishes or just casting off for an evening sail.

We had grown up on that lake. Learned to swim, sail, and fish there. Spent our summers in that water wearing matching but different-colored bathing suits.

Freddie is an excellent diver. She spent hours practicing off our dock, my dad in the water up to his neck, encouraging her. I used to watch how Freddie would bend her legs, how they would tense right before she pushed off, the way she kept her toes pointed as she hit the water.

She held my hand the first time I went to dive, our toes curled over the edge of the old wooden dock. When she let go, I sailed into the water. I knew what to do. I had learned all I needed to know from watching her.

Days and days went by when all we did was swim and lie on the dock, wrapping ourselves in our thick beach towels when the sun started to set, our hair still dripping from its sun-bleached ends.

My sisters were my best friends. We shared secrets, sandwiches, every minute of our lives, even a bathroom. I was jealous that Yorke got to sail in her little boat alone, that Freddie was taller than I was, that they both could French braid and do a perfect cartwheel. I spent all my time trying to catch up with them and measure up. I still do.

Roger took a tight curve. I reached up, fingers tangling in my hair, and settled back with Yorke's news, waiting for the familiar feeling of jealousy to kick in.

Every time we drove past our old house on our way to the club, my mother would insist we slow down so she could curse the new owners. "Geraniums. How common," she would comment, her eyes following the house, her head motionless. "Mason," she would say to my dad, "did you see the color of the shutters?"

With Roger behind the wheel, there was no slowing down for the lake house, even though flashes of it appeared between the trees and then disappeared as quickly as the memories running through my mind. There was no slowing down, period. Freddie and I were going to be lucky to get out of this drive with our kneecaps intact. Summer already seemed to be rushing by, and it hadn't even officially started yet.

Roger slammed to a stop at the club's curved

entry, and my knees smacked into Freddie's with a sick thud. Our bodies flung forward until our seat belts caught and tightened us down.

Roger was out in a flash, not having said a word the entire drive. It seemed he preferred to communicate nonverbally through erratic gearshifting and sudden, violent braking.

He was around to Yorke's side of the car with his hand on the door before the engine even stopped. He opened it gallantly, she stepped out and kissed him, then he pushed the seat forward and held the door for Freddie. I was left to fend for myself.

Struggling with my seat belt and my wind-whipped hair, I didn't notice the hand held out for me until it was right there in my face. It was not the large, lumbering hand of my boyfriend. It was masculine, yes, but in a thinner, more energetic, knuckle-cracking kind of way.

I glanced up into green eyes with bits of brown dancing in them as I shook my hair over my shoulder, rubbed my sore knee, grabbed my purse, and then reached for the outstretched hand.

"Smooth ride?" he asked. A smile curved up one side of his mouth.

I laughed. When he wrapped his fingers around mine, a warm current of electricity flowed through me. I felt suddenly solid, as if my world had been rolling past me and it had stopped, right now, amazingly sharp and in focus as if I had just taken off my roller skates. I didn't want to let go.

Roger appeared in front of us. His sharp creases and crisp lines were unaffected by his driving. His face was serious, and the key to the red M3 was swinging from one of his fingers. He dangled it and then finally dropped it. Those electric fingers snagged the key, breaking our hold, and my heart, midair.

"Keep it close," Roger requested as he leaned in to read the embroidered name on the red nylon club jacket. He clapped his hand down twice on the broad shoulder next to mine and said, "Porter," with a small smile and a folded five-dollar bill.

Then he cleared his throat, slid his hand up to check that his hair was at full attention, and proceeded to circle his entire car once, admiring and assessing it before he reached for Yorke again and pulled her across the warm blacktop toward the stairs leading up to the club.

I could feel Porter's green eyes on me as I crossed the parking lot, my sharp heels stabbing into the soft tar that had spent the day in the sun.

My face flushed and my pace quickened as I realized that at this moment I was not jealous of Yorke, not at all. Not of her engagement, or her huge diamond ring, and especially not of Roger, a man whose shoes and belt matched the interior of his car.

I reached the stairs and paused, burning a memory in my mind, one that was all mine, that didn't involve my sisters.

His eyes, the green so bright, the sideways smile, the way it felt when he held my hand. My fingers tingled still, and I wrapped them into a fist, trying to hold on tight.

"Hurry up," my sisters called out to me from

the entrance, and I followed after them, one step behind. It was Yorke, Freddie, and then me, like always, up the curved stairs and into the club.

My parents lean in to each other, looking like the picture-perfect, if a bit inebriated, married couple, and give each other a quick peck on the lips before dropping their napkins onto the cluttered table and rising out of their chairs.

It is time for them to make the rounds, to say hello to old friends, giving people a chance to congratulate them on Freddie's brilliance. Time to spread the news of Yorke and Roger's engagement.

The lights are low in the private alcove my mother reserved for this special family occasion, the knotty pine paneling and framed mallard and drake prints muted by the candlelight and windows swagged with thick velvet drapes.

"Ready or not, Leah," Shane says under his breath. Beneath the long dark tablecloth he clamps his thick hand over my knee with such force that my front teeth knock against my wineglass just as

I am taking a sip. I start steadying myself for the impending approach of my mother.

She's making her way down the table, kissing everyone as she passes behind our chairs. My dad is giving out handshakes like a politician to his shiny pink family now full of expensive steaks and red wine.

I set my glass down and shove my dinner plate away. The meat, red in the middle because that is the way my family eats it, is untouched.

Strings of summer squash dangle from the tines of my heavy sterling fork. I moved the carrots and fancy piped potatoes around on the plate but didn't manage to actually consume any of them.

My mother's hand, cool and smooth, presses lightly on my right shoulder when she arrives behind my chair. My head is heavy, sloshing full of wine, and I feel slightly trapped. I attempt to cover up my plate with my napkin, pulling the edges of the napkin down over the thick steak. I'm kind of a mess.

She leans down near my ear. She is an

intoxicating mix of Chanel No. 5, grilled meat, and merlot. "And next year?" she asks, her eyes locking on to mine meaningfully before she finishes her thought. "Should I expect to be up there again?"

She lifts her glass toward the head of the table, where my sisters, the engaged and the graduating, sit wrapped in dark plaid wallpaper and cozy candlelight.

Avoiding her gaze, I watch the wine in her glass swirl. It coats the inside of the crystal, like a good wine should, before slipping back down into the bowl.

"Let's not get ahead of ourselves," my dad says with a rumbling laugh when he arrives at my side at last.

I lean toward her, and she gives me a quick kiss on the cheek, dismissing me. My dad catches her up into the crook of his arm, his dark suit coat crinkling against her as he pulls her away.

Reaching over Shane, I grab the sweating silver ice bucket from the middle of the table and dangle it by its curved handles in front of my face. There it is:

the dreaded coral lip print. I smudge it off with the back of my hand, looking past my curved reflection to see my parents in miniature, disappearing hand in hand into the crowd of tan faces, highlighted hair, and friendly smiles.

I feel Shane's hand slip from my thigh as I lean forward to set the ice bucket back down and spy Freddie near the end of the long table, hovering over the blown-out candles and half-eaten cake. Thick chocolate slabs are missing, but yellow roses still sit primly around the edges. It's just like our driveway, but in cake form. Freddie is calm and amazingly composed, considering that Yorke is stealing her hard-earned graduation thunder with an overstarched, shrub-haired frat boy and a diamond ring. I guess she's had a lot of practice at being second.

"Congrats, Freddie," I yell in her direction. She lifts her rosy face, and we raise our glasses toward each other. I down mine in one, the wine amplifying my pride and my volume.

Shane pushes back from the table, his plate

scraped clean, decorative garnishes and all. He grabs a bottle from the middle of the table and refills my glass with the dregs. Chucking the spent bottle upside down into the silver bucket with a splash, he holds up his empty glass and tips it back and forth in my direction, his fingers looking freakishly large on the thin stem.

"Shall we?" he asks.

Knowing we will need adults for any possible refills, he is eager to stay close to my parents. I nod and stand too quickly, my brain filling with booze until I slide sideways against the overstuffed country club chair and find myself sitting again, hands resting in my lap.

Shane reaches for me. I put my fingers in his, feeling no electricity, no warm tingling, just the calluses and rough skin left over from his championship baseball season. I let him pull me up.

"Hey, Rog," Shane yells as soon as I am steady. His hand presses on the small of my back as we walk toward the end of the table. "I haven't had the chance to congratulate you personally."

Their hands meet like two leather baseball mitts, and Yorke looks ready to burst. You can tell they are measuring each other up. Looking at Roger's trim pinstriped suit and gelled bangs, I hope Shane wins.

Yorke reaches past Roger to hug me, maneuvering her way to get closer to the open dining room and the masses that haven't heard about her impending marriage.

She squeezes me halfheartedly with one arm, and her drink, brimming with mint and ice, drips down my back, soaking my dress and my hair. She lets go quickly, grabs Roger, and leads him away. She smiles back at me over her shoulder, dangling her drink in one hand and Roger in the other, before melting into a sea of sparkling silverware and well-fed families.

I feel my hair lying damp and sticky against my back. Thanks, Yorke. I lean over to wipe my fingers on the soft linen tablecloth.

"I am going to—" I start explaining to Shane, but he is busy dragging a chair across the classic tartan carpet, pulling in close to Freddie with a big smile on his face, his teeth stained dark and grayish by the wine. He holds his empty glass out in front of him like it's some red plastic cup he paid three dollars for at a keg party.

Freddie and Evan are still sitting at the end of our table. Leaning in very close to each other, speaking in French, they are lost deep in a conversation. They have been in advanced languages together since the first semester of their freshman year, seriously dating since the second. Oblivious to Shane and the fact that they are huddling around the last bottle of wine and it's at least half full, their voices lilt and trill above the din. I wish Shane luck, knowing that the best he can do in French is a butchered version of "*Je joue au tennis*," and head off for the bathroom.

As I pass the buffet near the front door, I swipe a handful of the pastel-colored dinner mints usually reserved for alcoholics and small children. I pull out the pink ones and drop the rest into a potted plant.

For years, at the end of every Friday night family dinner, I have secretly gobbled them down. The first time they appeared on the buffet near the host stand, mounded up in that silver tray with a tiny silver caviar spoon, they sparkled at me like little candy diamonds. Yorke, bold even at eight, stepped right up and scooped a small spoonful for all of us to share. They were three perfect shades of pastel, just like us.

Huddled in a tight circle in a pool of light in the parking lot, we stretched out our hands and discovered that they were not blue, yellow, and pink, like our matching dresses. They were, under closer inspection, *green*, yellow, and pink, practically perfect but not close enough for Yorke. She threw hers down onto the pavement with a loud "Those are for babies!" and stomped off to the car, the heels of her little blue dress shoes clacking loudly along the blacktop.

The green candies bounced away, out of the circle of light that had given them up as impostors, and rolled off into the dark, lost under the bellies of our friends' and neighbors' cars.

I knew those candies weren't for babies. I also

knew that Yorke wouldn't eat them just because they weren't blue, her signature color, and that there was *no* way Freddie would eat the yellow ones, not now.

I watched Freddie drop hers one by one on our way to the car, like a trail of bread crumbs on the blacktop. I held on to mine tight when my dad scooped me up and put me in the car, and I clung to them all the way home. Even though they leave your teeth kind of fuzzy and make your breath even worse, I have been eating them on the sly ever since.

In fair weather the dining room at our club opens up to a humongous wooden deck that overlooks the golf course and, beyond that, the lake. I veer to the left onto the deck when I should be veering to the right and into the ladies' room.

I step out into the evening air, and the sun is right now making its last stab at daytime, painting the sky the same bright pinks, oranges, and reds that flood Freddie's bedroom.

Leaning up against the railing, my hair still damp and my glass still almost full, I take a sip and wonder if Paris really does look like a sunset or if that is just Freddie's interpretation. I guess I will find out eventually.

I'll probably go abroad like Freddie. My French is not nearly as good as hers, but Freddie had to overdo it like she always does and master the language in one semester. I don't have much interest in French, really. When I was picking classes for my freshman year, I had to pick a language, and both my sisters had studied French, so it seemed like the way to go.

I didn't realize it might lead to something someday, like actual French conversations or a trip to France. I am not sure if I even like French people. I am fond of shaved armpits. I detest stinky cheese. And I am pretty sure my hair won't work with a beret.

Yorke didn't go abroad, but she did get engaged to Roger. Hmm . . . nine months of smelling armpits on crowded European streets or a lifetime with a man who just might trim his hair with a hedge clipper. There must be another option.

I turn around, resting an elbow on the railing, and look through the floor-to-ceiling glass windows that run the length of the dining room, searching the crowd for my sisters. The setting sun bounces off all the sterling, crystal, and glass. I narrow my eyes against the glare.

There they are, standing side by side, talking to the lady that lived next door to us at the lake house.

I move myself to the right until my reflection fits in and joins them. There is my hair, my smile, the way my hand covers my mouth when I laugh, my ability to make chocolate chip cookies, my best back tuck, the dress I am wearing right now, the pride I should feel when I am named valedictorian, and the sparkle I will have when wearing my engagement ring for the first time.

Gazing through that window, I see my sisters reflecting my past and presenting a prefolded map of my future. No need for me to open it up and navigate. I can simply follow the path they have laid out for me.

I drain the rest of my drink, the tannins biting at the back of my tongue. I shift, then turn and walk away, leaving my sisters and an empty glass behind me.

❤ ❤ ❤

Somewhere down around the seventeenth hole, where the driveway curves in pretty close and almost hugs the fairway, I see the M3 speeding smoothly along in the distance, its bright redness moving through the cultivated green of the golf course.

Walking slowly through the soft, short grass, my sandals hanging loosely in my hand, I stop and watch it slow down before it whips a quick U-turn and heads back toward the club.

I hear it roaring toward me over the last hill. I align my toes along the edge of the asphalt drive and wait for Roger, trimmed and pressed, to squeal to a stop in front of me.

The car rolls up and comes to an easy, effortless stop at the tip of my toes. It's Porter. His wild brown hair sticks up all over his head, thick and messy, and his green eyes look me up and down, burning through me, finally resting on my bare feet.

I tip my head to the side, fingers lost in my hair, already twisting as I ask, "What are you doing?"

Not the smoothest of lines, but I am surprised to see him there, his hands looking so familiar as they rest along the top of Roger's steering wheel.

"Keeping it close," he says as if it were obvious. He smiles that crooked smile again and stretches his long arms out far and wide around the interior of the car, almost grazing the passenger door with his fingertips.

I feel bolted to the ground.

"Umm . . . " I flick my hair over my shoulder and eye the clubhouse, a couple of greens behind us. "I think he meant close to the building."

It is just dark enough that the candles on the tables in the main dining room have been lit. They look like fireflies caught in a really big jar.

"Nah," he says, shaking his head, very sure of himself. "I think he meant me. Keep it close to me."

"Highly unlikely," I say, dropping my hand.

Shaking the loose broken hair from around my fingers, I look him straight in those sparkling green eyes and make the understatement of the century— "Roger is pretty attached to this car."

"I can see why."

He revs the engine a couple of times.

"This car is hot." He drags the word out with a slight southern twang so it sounds more like *hhhawt* and leans forward to rub the dash in a very possessive way.

I watch, mesmerized, expecting to see a streak of phosphorescence trailing behind his fingers.

"Want a ride?" he asks.

I laugh, because I am not that easy. But God, do I want to say yes.

I realize I am still watching his hands. I don't know what I am waiting for, but I can't stop staring. I snap my head up and drag my eyes away.

I shake my head and say, "I've been there before," with a nod toward the backseat.

"True," he agrees. He rests his chin on the tips of his fingers as if he is solving an equation and breathes in quickly, the solution found. "But not with me," he says.

My first impulse is to move toward him like a sex-starved teenage zombie, arms out, neck exposed. But I can't. I look away from him, my eyes drawn back toward the club and the lights flickering from inside. Want to. Can't.

"Thanks," I say, refusing him as politely as I can with another shake of my head.

Dropping my sandals over my right shoulder, I hold tight to the thin leather straps and start making my way back toward the clubhouse.

"Your choice," he says with a shrug as he puts the car into gear and rolls away slowly. Superslowly.

So slowly he paces me, one hand comfortably slung over the steering wheel, his green eyes watching my every move as I walk along the side of the road.

I turn and watch him too, crossing one arm over my chest, bare feet soft and silent in the grass, trying to look unfazed by the challenge.

One side of his mouth lifts, and he gives me that crooked smile, making the wine flush on my cheeks even pinker. He stops the car. I walk toward the door, my steps light, our eyes locked. My fingertips brush against the cool silver of the door handle, and suddenly it's ripped away from me. I gasp and yank my hand back as Porter speeds off.

He squawks to a stop about five feet away and tries to look nonchalant. He slides his arm along the curved back of the passenger seat, turns toward me, and waits patiently as I cover the ground between us on foot.

I reach for the door again, tensed, ready to pull back at the first sign of movement, mentally accepting the possibility that my fingers are about to be removed by force.

Porter revs the engine, watching me closely. I hear the sound of the cylinders making their upward climb again, and I go for it, grabbing the handle. I scrabble, pull the door open, toss my sandals onto the floor, and heave myself into the car, all arms and long blond hair and boobs escaping from my strapless dress as I crawl onto the seat, breathing like a maniac.

I look up from my undignified, hunkered spot and see Porter facing me, grinning appreciatively, my boobs practically in his face, his arm still resting lightly along the back of my seat.

The car never moved. Damn, he got me.

"Nice entrance." He smiles, slipping his left hand onto the wheel, the other one leaving the back of my seat to reach down and put the car into gear.

"I've been working on it," I say breathlessly, following his green eyes to my cleavage, which is spilling out everywhere, practically filling the car with soft white flesh.

With a faint smile, I pull up at the top of my dress while I pull down on the hem and simultaneously turn around in my seat to face forward. Porter steps on the gas, and we are gone, streaking down the road, away from the lingering lights of the club, and off, into the night.

Later, back inside the M3 with my head leaning against the leather headrest, I watch the dark golf course roll by. I am surrounded by my sisters, the air is warm, the location familiar, yet I feel off course, no longer on the map.

My eyes are trained on the horizon, on the slight rise just off the twelfth hole, to the left of the green. I wait impatiently, wishing Roger would drive faster, so I can see the exact spot.

I think I might be holding my breath, because I know that there, just off the green, invisible from the road but burned vividly into my memory, under a large oak with branches that covered us like a canopy, there are imprints, the grass flattened into crop circles by our bodies.

Squinting through the darkness, I smile as we cruise by. I close my eyes and sink down, remembering the cool grass, soft and springy beneath my head as I rolled onto my back. Porter was splayed out next to me. My face and lips were red, hot, swollen, and a bit bruised. He leaned up on one elbow and lowered his head down to mine, ready for more.

"You smell like mint," he had whispered as his lips grazed past my ear, teasing me.

I arched up as I kissed him, his tongue slid smoothly into my mouth, and my brain raced to keep up, to stay in control. I was pulled under again, awash in the sensations, lost.

My fingers had curled into the grass beneath

me, as his fingers trailed lightly down my arm, his touch leaving a throbbing current, flowing from soft inner elbow to wrist.

I was breathing fast, hot against his neck. Then I leaned my neck back as he kissed me from under the curve of my chin to the top of my dress, and his hand no longer rested solidly on my stomach but gently pressed up, pushing what was already almost falling out the top of my dress to the very edge.

I felt his tongue graze along my hot skin there, and I struggled against the rising tide and came up for air. I pushed up against him and pushed him away. Porter rolled off me, flat onto his back, arms flung out to the sides with his face to the sky. Panting.

I am not the type of girl to do something like that. It is not in my nature. I was prom queen last year. I will be homecoming queen in the fall. Both my sisters were. I date the captain of the football team, just like Yorke and my mother, too, when she was in school. I'd like to say I have a lock on the whole valedictorian thing next year, but with Valerie around, I am keeping my fingers crossed.

I don't need to drive off in a suspiciously borrowed car and end up making out with some random guy. It was a whole year before I even let Shane put his hand up my shirt. He tried many, many times, and I fought him off, protecting my turf against what I knew would be an inevitable march forward. It's boobs first, then down the pants, undies off, and then, after that, everything is fair game.

We spend late Friday nights and most Saturday afternoons scrimmaging in my bed, above the sheets, with Shane slowly gaining ground. But what my boyfriend spent more than twelve months achieving inch by inch in my bedroom, Porter had plundered in a few sweaty minutes on the fairway near the twelfth hole.

I had lain there, looking up at a sky so blue it was almost black, listening to Porter's breathing as it returned to normal, feeling mine finally slowing, too. All those weekends and tangled after-school specials with Shane, combined, added up, and totaled, did not feel as good as this one brief grassy smash with Porter. I felt like I just got a big drink of water when I didn't even know I was thirsty. It was so good it scared the shit out of me.

"Leah . . ." Freddie says softly from the snug seat next to me, her voice bringing me back to the car, to the warm night rolling past me, but I am unable to turn my head and drag my eyes away from the fairway until I feel her hand on my shoulder.

"Leah," she says again, a little louder this time, with a small, surprised laugh, "you've got grass in your hair."

She runs her fingers lightly through my hair and holds out a few blades. She drops them, long and green, into my palm, and I close my hand around them, running my knuckles softly against my bruised lips, searching for the scent of mint between my curved fingers.

Freddie is watching me closely. Yorke looks over her shoulder, glancing back from the front seat with her eyes wide.

I open my hand. The grass is a striking green against my pale palm as we pass under an amber streetlamp, as green as Porter's eyes. Roger shifts into gear, and a breeze drops down, swirling through the convertible. It lifts the grass up and blows it away. I watch it disappear. My sisters look away as I lower my hand and slowly settle back into place.

Three

My family, all experts in reading my mother's moods, disappears as soon as we get home from the gymnasium. My sisters split off in different directions, shadowed by their boyfriends. Freddie, the first one across the foyer, slips up the steps, still in her cap and gown, defecting to her Parisian bedroom with Evan.

Seconds later I hear "*Pour aimer . . . pour avoir aimé . . . être aimé . . .*" as the sound of Gérard, the well-modulated voice on Freddie's language tapes, floats down the stairs.

Freddie has been Frenching it up all day. All morning long we heard the tensing of French verbs, while Yorke covered the dining room table with bridal magazines and crowded me (and the last few Os in my cereal bowl) right out of the room, and while I stepped out of the shower and Freddie yanked our bathroom door open to find her favorite lip gloss—excuse me, *son brillant à lèvres*—then left me steaming on the bath mat.

My mother had tensed right along with Gérard, her mood notching up slowly from breakfast through to lunch, reaching a fevered pitch as we rushed back home after Freddie's graduation ceremony with, according to her, "a thousand things to do before all the guests arrive" and the party officially got under way.

Yorke circles the staircase the long way and sneaks out back to join Roger and my dad in the rented white tent, leaving Shane and me alone with my mother, and she is closing in behind us.

I grab Shane's hand and bound up the stairs two at a time, climbing away from the sound of her heels clicking furiously across the Italian tile and her voice calling, "Be back down here in fifteen minutes!"

Fourteen minutes and thirty seconds later I am flat on my back, soft flowered sheets rumpling up against my skin, bra off, and legs twisting around the duvet.

"Shane," I whisper as his head lowers and his lips nudge away at the neck of my T-shirt. "Shane . . ." I say again, feeling his hand, too warm on my stomach, slowly making its way upward. He breathes back, his only response a slight arching of his neck to come at me at a better angle.

I reach around his back, squeezing hard as I try to see the clock on my dresser behind his head. His hands feel heavy, my hair is caught somewhere, and I am so warm and suffocated and tired.

I don't know what I was thinking, dragging him up here, hoping to feel some spark, to thrash about hot and heavy as if we were on green, soft grass, with the night open and smooth around us. I thought maybe something had changed for me last night. That I had woken up somehow.

I push at his hands, wanting them to stop moving in careless, wandering circles, wanting nothing but air and coolness between us.

"Shane! Leah! Get down here!" my mother screams, and I can almost hear her bracelets against the banister.

"Shit," Shane says into my neck before his head snaps up and his eyes crack open, lids heavy against the early-afternoon sun streaming through my windows. "So much for the French lessons."

He rolls off me and stands quickly, smoothing out the front of his long khaki shorts and flicking his bangs to the side.

"Let's go," he says impatiently with his eyes on the unlocked door.

"I can't go like this," I say, still lying on the bed, pointing at my blue T-shirt, all stretched out and twisted, my boobs free and naked underneath. "Julia would not be pleased."

I sit up and search around in the tangled duvet. I find my bra and start to put it on, sliding it under my shirt.

"Hook this thing, Shane," I say with my chin down and my fingers foreign and clumsy behind my back.

Shane of course bypasses the bra completely and reaches for my goods.

"Jesus, Shane." I swear through clenching teeth as I fight him off.

Kneeling, I swing my hair over my shoulder and feel a section that clings, still damp and sweaty, to the back of my neck.

I reach back and try again. "She is going to walk in the door any second."

"I am much better at the unhooking part," Shane says in frustration, but he twists my lacy pink bra around in his football fingers until he gets it hooked.

Shane and I have barely touched down on the last step when there my mother is, pushing a large silver vase overflowing with yellow tea roses into my arms.

"Find somewhere to put these where Freddie can enjoy them," she says as she walks off toward the kitchen.

Caterers are carrying more of everything in through the garage door. A constant stream of aproned workers, steaming silver pans, and large, Saran-covered platters passes through the arched doorway.

Right, I think, holding the flowers out and away from me at arm's length as I search the room for a place to stash them. I was there when Freddie had a couple of accidents and Yorke invented pee-your-bed yellow. Freddie has shunned yellow ever since, but my mother keeps trying.

I set the flowers down on a small trestle table in our family room and feel a slip and a slosh. Water drips onto my fingers and the polished wood tabletop.

"Oh, and Fred . . . Lee . . . Yorke," my mother calls impatiently.

Finally she is out of choices and lands on "Leah."

Her head pops around the corner, and she finds me wiping my wet hands on my already used-looking T-shirt.

"Go change," she says, eyeing me up and down

with a disquieting glance. "It's almost time and you look . . . disheveled."

God, she doesn't even know which one I am. She just knows I don't look good enough.

I retreat across the foyer with Shane in tow. He's so close he's practically in my back pocket as I grab the railing at the base of the stairs.

My mother's slender fingers slide onto his forearm, stopping us both.

"Shane," she says with a smooth smile, the coral tips of her fingers denting into his skin, "won't you come give me a hand at the bar?"

She peels him away from me, and I head back to my room alone, feeling mostly pissed at her, but also a little thankful, because for once I can climb the stairs without Shane hotboxing me step by step.

I kneel on my bed and push the window open, letting in a breeze that floats my sheer white curtains. Leaning back on my heels, I breathe deeply as the smell of Shane, a combination of spicy cologne and gym locker, fades away.

Opening the louvered doors of my walk-in closet,

I hit the light and step inside to find something to wear that my mother will deem appropriate.

I flick the hangers, sliding summer dresses, tank tops, skirts, and jeans past my view. I make it all the way to the end, past the stuff I haven't worn since freshman year and the stuff with tags still on it that I will never wear because my mother has picked it out for me while shopping with her girlfriends, and then I look at everything again, sliding the velvet padded hangers back the other way.

Nothing seems right. I pull my skirt off and kick it to the back of the closet, then drop my T onto the heap of dirty clothes piled next to my laundry basket. It lands on top of the short black dress I wore last night.

I pick the dress up and press the dark, soft jersey to my face, instantly smelling my perfume and hair spray. I breathe in even deeper and smell mint and—this just might be my imagination—the green, fresh smell of grass.

I walk up to the full-length mirror propped up against the wall. Holding the black dress in front of me, I crook the side of my mouth up and smile back at my reflection, just to see how it looks. Then a smile—a real, true Leah smile—breaks out on my face and my choice is clear. It's not exactly clean, and I know my mother knows I was wearing it last night because she was wearing the old lady version of it herself and my sisters had on almost exact duplicates, except theirs were just a bit shorter and tighter, but right now I really want to wear this dress.

I spring up onto my bed and peer out the window, holding the black dress tightly against my chest. I kneel, resting my butt on my heels, and look down over the yard.

The sun is bright, shimmering in wavy diamonds on top of the just-cleaned pool water, highlighting the curves of the glasses that are lined up neatly behind the bar.

Little round tables draped in white linen dot the lawn. A bowlful of my mother's yellow roses sits atop every flat surface big enough to hold one, drawing my eye from post to post and table to table, a blooming dot-to-dot across our freshly cut yard.

Yellow streamers decorate the fence. Yellow balloons are tied to the tent poles. Our whole yard is pee-your-bed yellow.

Our back gate opens. A big yellow bow is tied to the top. It swings back and forth as the first guests arrive and the party gets under way.

Freddie and my mother step up, with my dad right behind them, to greet the guests. I watch my family taking their places, lining up to say hello and how are you, it's great to see you, and thanks so much for coming.

Freddie gets the kisses and congratulations, for now, but I'm sure Yorke will bust that up as soon as she can. As if on cue, I watch my mother lift her arm and wave Yorke over from the shade of the rented tent.

The guests are coming in thick, practically lining up behind the gate.

Yorke's sandals clack across the patio as she takes her spot, maneuvering Roger, dark and slim, into place behind her and up to the right a little, like a flat key on a piano.

I have a bird's-eye view, but I already know it by heart. It's the same in every picture we have ever posed for—in the snapshots that fill the thick leather photo albums and in the black-and-white portraits inside the hefty sterling silver frames that line the walls and cover every mantelpiece of our house.

It used to be that my mother would guide us into place, my dad waiting patiently off to the side with the tripod and the flash.

"Yorke is first 'cause she is the oldest," my mother would say, "then Freddie, and finally Leah."

Her fingertips would dig into our shoulders as she arranged us, blue, yellow, and pink, to her satisfaction. Then she would step back and admire her work and say something like "That's one for our Christmas card," as my dad snapped away.

I rest my forehead against the windowpane. I can see where I am supposed to fit. There is a spot waiting for me at the end of the line. Freddie and Yorke know how to set it up now, no guidance necessary. Today is the garden party version. My sisters are shades of cool summer, icy blue, soft sea green, and long blond hair. I drop the black dress, crushing it under my knees, knowing what is expected of me, knowing the dress won't work.

Outside, the pile of cards and gifts continues to grow. The chatter of the guests and the tinkling of glass rise up toward me like a thunderhead building over the yard as I try to see beyond our neatly trimmed hedge, my pulse raising, hoping for a flash of bright red, a car rolling up to take me away from the careful orchestration that is my life. But I know that car is carefully parked in front of our house, in the shade to keep the soft leather seats from the sun.

Last night was the most fun that car and I have probably ever had. We went out, polished and prepared for a standard Friday night, a smooth ride, no bumps in the road. But we came back different. Our engines had been run out. Revved up. Roger had only to slide the M3's driver's seat forward to get things back to normal. I don't know what it's going to take for me.

Below me, my mother leans forward to kiss one of my dad's golfing buddies on the cheek and notices the break in the line. Her line. Her unhappiness is immediately apparent as she leans back, tightening up, her bracelets glinting when they slide silently down her arm, their metallic clink lost in the sounds of the swelling party.

She folds her arms tightly across her chest, and her smile disappears for a split second, her mouth becoming a sharp slash of coral. I can almost feel her hands on my shoulders, sliding me into place.

My throat tightens, and I scramble down off the bed. I grab the first pink dress I can find, pull it on, and hurry down the stairs to complete my mother's matching set.

You can see the sweat rolling down Evan's face even though it's already pretty dark. He's behind Freddie, doing some kind of bump and grind thing, as she sways to the music, eyes closed, the gold honor cords she received earlier today sliding slowly from her neck.

A miniature disco ball hangs over them. It spins and twinkles, illuminating the sprigs of grass sprouting up around the edges of the rented floor.

Lights from the black-draped DJ table tint Evan's hardworking face in a wash of colors as he makes his moves, the center of attention on the dance floor. He is getting into it, hips shaking, arms raised, clapping to the beat some of the time, but mostly missing it completely.

I feel a little bad for Evan. Grossed out mostly, because of the sweating, but also a bit bad because he is on the kill list and doesn't even realize it. If he did, I doubt he would be putting this much energy into some old eighties song.

No Johnson sister escapes to college with a high school boyfriend holding her back. Evan is on his way out, the same way Yorke's high school boyfriend Dwight was the summer she graduated. The same way Shane will be a year from now.

"Let's dance," Shane says, stretching his arm out along the back of my chair, his breath malty and thick in my ear as he rubs my shoulder. He has been pawing at me and rubbing around on me all day.

"Come on," he says, his fingers, sticky with beer, making a clumsy circle on my bare skin, "let's go."

Figuring Shane is a lot like a dog and if I don't make eye contact he will eventually lose interest and pant away, I don't even look at him. I keep my eyes glued on Freddie and Evan.

You can tell that Evan just wants to get into Freddie's pants. That he just knows that since she is pretty drunk and it is a special occasion, he is in there. Right, I think, stripping Shane's fingers off my shoulder, one by one, hoping he will get the hint, dead man dancing.

A little slow on the uptake, as usual, Shane finally moves his arm. He swirls his smuggled beer around in a dainty white coffee cup and finishes it off in a big gulp, oblivious of the fact that I am walking away, the ground squishing under my heels as I escape.

It has been a rush of relatives and old friends and fancy little appetizers washed down with well-wishes all day. With Shane's arm looped around my waist, the warm sun melting us together like chocolates, we lined up with my family, and I smiled and answered the same questions over and over and over.

"Will you go abroad next year just like Freddie?" I would be asked.

I don't know, my brain would think.

"Of course she will," my mother would answer.

"Can we expect another valedictorian next year?"

I would nod and smile, thinking, Of course you can. Mr. Hobart's got it all arranged.

Then they would lean into each other as they walked away, saying the same thing everybody says, "She's just like her sisters."

Can people even tell us apart, or do they only know it's me 'cause I am at the end of the line?

I turn back toward the tent. Little girls dance right next to the towering black DJ speakers, their hands clasped, their cheeks pink and bright.

The music fades, and the girls keep bouncing, their shiny little dress shoes reflecting the lights. My mother stands in the middle of the dance floor. My dad, straightening his tie, rushes over to join her.

"Everyone," my mother says, squinting into the light with her hand over her brow, like a ship captain searching for land.

"Everyone," she repeats, more loudly this time and in a higher pitch as her gaze slides from the ancient relatives in the way back to the little dancers at her feet.

She waits for the calm.

She raises a glass, and the hem of her dress inches a modest amount up her thigh as she says, "Please join us in a toast."

I watch Freddie swirl to a stop in the corner of the dance floor. She steadies herself, smoothing back her hair and adjusting the gold cords around her neck.

"It is our honor," my mother declares, turning to look at my dad with an expression of absolute pride.

"Our pleasure," he chimes in, his head bowing toward hers, the golden bubbles alight in his raised glass of beer.

"To announce the engagement of our daughter Yorke—" my mother says over delighted gasps. The sound of thunderous clapping lifts the sides of the tent and drowns out the rest of her toast and any mention of Roger, who is standing at attention at Yorke's side.

I see Freddie slump, but it lasts for only a second. She rebounds quickly, Johnson style, storing her anger and smoothing it over with a smile and a hug from the toothy boyfriend at her side.

She looks great, but I know she is falling apart, her moment in the sun being stolen clap by clap and kiss by kiss as Yorke starts her victory lap.

It's like the year Yorke got a new bike on Freddie's birthday. The day belonged to Freddie, but Yorke drove away with it on a pearly white three-speed with silver streamers dangling from the handlebars. Freddie got a bike, too, but nobody seemed to notice.

I step back into the tent and make my way toward

Freddie, accidentally getting too close to a tableful of relatives. Before I can slip past, they begin a fresh round of "You must be so proud" and "Just think, next year it will be you," distracting me from Freddie and her distress.

In the small space of time it takes me to disentangle myself from their polite hugs and paper-thin kisses, Freddie has completely regained her composure.

My sisters are hugging and twirling together in the middle of the dance floor, Yorke's smile and engagement ring sparkling, Freddie's blond hair and honor cords swinging in a gold blur.

I lean kind of indecently past some old man wearing a bow tie and a cardigan that only someone really old and possibly close to death could wear on a hot summer night like this and snag a glass of, hopefully, untouched beer. I raise it in a silent toast. It's not as if Freddie were the first valedictorian in this family, but considering that Yorke's class was a bunch of dumbasses, she certainly was the best.

I drink to her, knowing that with Yorke around, she will never get to be the first at anything. Or, I realize, the beer bubbling in my brain, the last. So I drink to all three of us.

Four

The last three days of school drip by. The parties, the yearbook signings, even the final class photos feel uneventful. I am listless, wilted, my pulse slow and slippery like water in a garden hose that's been left in the sun.

There is no breeze or breathing room at home. And our kitchen table is the front line in a silent war, France versus the traditional wedding. A bunker of bridal magazines flanks the left side of the breakfast nook, A *Guidebook to French Phrases* and an unfolded map of the Paris Métro dominate the right, leaving the silver salt and pepper shakers unprotected in the middle of no-man's-land on the flowered tablecloth.

It appears that the wedding is winning, hands down. It has strong support, being fully backed by my mother. It is easy for her to get behind a good wedding. She understands a world full of beautiful dresses and guest lists. France, however, she doesn't get. She's never been.

It took Freddie months of prodding and convincing—plus an unexpected phone call during dinner one night last spring from Madame Lesac, promoting Freddie's fluency and exceptional French skills—to get permission for a year abroad.

But it was a comment from our new next-door neighbor, who had spent a summer in France before college and declared it to be a "perfectly civilized place," that finally got my mother to cave and laid the groundwork for this breakfast nook battle, where there are apparently no skirmishes, just lots of tension. Sitting between the warring factions each morning, I am usually shell-shocked before I can even finish my orange juice.

It's 9:00 A.M. on June 5, my first official day of summer, and already it is eighty-eight degrees. I hit the hill that leads down into the park, the hardest part of my long walk to the public pool, and adjust my backpack, feeling a bubble of heat escape from underneath it, even though the sun is still low in the sky.

I follow the path that circles the flower garden, where the air smells sweet and buzzes with fat bumblebees. Flowers already trying to avoid the wilting sun lean over and box me in, bumping along the top of my backpack.

When we were little, this park was one of our favorite places in the world. The flowers were so tall and dense back then that you could get lost and disappear in them. One time I looked up from my inspection of a bright red ladybug and saw only flowers. No sisters, no parents, not even a dog, only stems and leaves and petals that towered above me, closing in on each side.

I thought I was lost forever, alone in a forest of flowers. I stayed still, squatting next to my ladybug friend with my heart thumping and my eyes wide until the sound of my sisters laughing floated by.

I followed their voices, my little legs pumping until I promptly bumped into Yorke's back. There they were, just around a curve in the path, and I was safe.

I follow that same curve today, out of the flowerbed and back toward the street. Hitching my sliding backpack up again, I look up and notice a dark green Corvette slinking along the side of the road. I slow myself when the car rolls to a stop. I can almost feel someone watching me from behind its dark-tinted windows. I look around, nervously hoping to see Freddie and Yorke busting out of the tall flowers, just a step away as always, but the park is deserted.

The car idles, motionless, and then suddenly rumbles off down the hill as I stand watching, with my head cocked and my pulse racing.

Relieved and a little embarrassed, I silently scold myself for being such a chicken and start walking again. My mother is so worried about strangers that I think I have become paranoid. We know everyone in this town, for Christ's sake. There are no surprises around here.

Except for maybe that one, I think as I reach the bottom of the steep hill minutes later, the fronts of my thighs screaming. The dark green Corvette is parked at the bottom of the hill, the front tires pointing into the street, ready for a quick getaway, the engine still running. I see long legs in frayed jeans, a black T, messy brown hair, and those eyes. They glow green and sharp even in the bright morning light.

I stop, mid-step. I'm sure I look stupid. My mouth is hanging open, and my hair is pulled back in a sweaty ponytail. My mother would be so upset with me: I don't even have lipstick on. God, I can't believe I made out with this guy and I don't even know him.

His grin cracks open, and he asks, "Why are you

out walking so early on such a fine morning?"

I step closer, despite myself.

"Why are you out stalking me so early on such a fine morning?" I ask, figuring, as my dad always says, a good defense is the best offense, or whatever. I'm sure it can work for boys as well as football.

"I am not stalking you," he says with a definite emphasis on the "not."

"Are you sure?" I ask, raising my eyebrows before I turn to glance back up the hill. "It kind of felt like it."

"I wasn't sure it was you," he says, and then ducks his head to stare at his feet.

He actually looks kind of embarrassed when he reaches up and rakes his fingers through his hair.

He looks back up at me.

"You look different," he says. He grins again, and the heavens open up. "Very shiny."

"Thanks," I say while holding out one of my arms for him to admire. It is, like the rest of me, coated in a thick layer of SPF 30. I look as if I have been dipped in butter, but I smell like the beach.

"It's for work," I tell him.

"Where's that?"

"Up at the pool," I say, nodding in the direction of the pool. You can't see the water from where we are standing, just the top of the chain-link fence.

His eyes follow mine across the park as I continue. "I'm a lifeguard."

"Really?" he asks, grinning in a wicked way. He pauses for a beat. "You sure you're not just working on your tan?"

Now, this pisses me off, because a lot of people, Yorke, most of my friends, even this dude apparently, think that I am just going through the motions of lifeguarding so I can soak up some sun. If I were, wouldn't I at least wear a bikini? Or, better yet, sunbathe at home?

Thing is, my parents made me quit the swim team the summer before I started high school. I came downstairs that first day of vacation, ready for tryouts, knowing I was going to make the team, that trying out was just a formality for me since I had been on the team the summer before, and then my dad, sitting at the table, eating a boiled egg with a tiny spoon, commented on my shoulders. How big they were from all that backstroke.

My mother appeared, turned me around for a good look at my lats, and agreed. My shoulders were looking boyish.

Next thing you know, I am not swimming anymore. I am sitting on a tall metal chair with a whistle, watching little kids dog-paddle and fat people float.

That made it hurt exponentially. Lifeguarding was a compromise I made with my dad. I think he knew he broke my heart, or at least my swimming spirit, when they forced me to quit, so we struck a deal.

"Yes, I'm sure," I say with an exasperated sigh, planting my hand on my hip. "They wouldn't give me a whistle for that."

Shrugging, he puts his hands up in front of him as if he had clearly meant no offense.

"True," he says. "But you are a country club girl. Surely you can see how I might have been led astray."

"True," I say, twisting my toe into the tall sprigs of grass at the edge of the road, "but only on Friday nights. The rest of the summer I'll be slumming it down at the public pool."

He laughs, quiet and low.

"Well," he says as he turns away and pulls the car door open, "maybe I'll stop by sometime and say hi."

I fidget, not wanting him to go.

I should have just shut up and kissed him or something. He looks back at me.

I smile and nod, lifting my chin toward the small hill where the pool sits. "I'll be the one in the tall chair," I say. "In the red suit. In case you're not sure again."

"I'll look for the whistle," he says with a smile.

He gets into the car, sinking down into the low seat, and leans his elbow out the open window.

"But," he says, "you didn't answer my original question."

"Which was?" I ask.

"Why are you walking?"

"Easy," I say, flipping my backpack onto my

shoulder as he revs the engine. It grumbles low and deep. "I don't drive."

He looks away while he drops the car into drive, stops, and turns toward me to clarify.

"Don't drive or can't drive?" he asks, his brows knitting together.

"What's the difference?" I ask.

He extends his arm out the open window, palm up, as he thinks. His hand drops down and rests lightly against the car door.

"One is an aversion," he says, finally, "the other, a lack of ability."

I mull that over, never having given it much thought before. All the choices necessary when you are behind the wheel pop into my head. Right or left? Top up or down? Fast or slow? Ugh. It's easier to let someone else drive, to make those decisions for me.

"My lack of ability causes an aversion," I decide.

He nods. "We'll have to see if we can fix that."

My heart runs faster than the V-8 engine idling underneath him.

"You want a ride?" he asks.

I shrug.

"Your call," he says.

He gives me one last smile and squeals off, leaving me standing in the middle of the street, swirling in a cloud of elation, exhaust, and confusion.

The view from my lifeguard chair is good. I can see the entire park, which is the social hub of this tiny town in the summer months, from up here. I can see the thin two-lane road that widens into a parking lot next to the park store. The road circles the edge of the ball diamonds and comes back around to the shaded picnic shelters and worn wooden playgrounds, before climbing up the steep hill again on its way out of the park. A long, paved loop, this road strings the summer sports—baseball, T-ball, tennis, and swimming—together on a hot, black asphalt chain.

The crowd in the park is pretty light today, but it is early, in the day and in the season. I don't ever really expect to see anyone I know here, since they spend their summers at the lake or the club or some educational immersion camp.

Even the pool is fairly empty, despite the heat. A couple of young swimmers are crossing the width of the pool with very shaky strokes, pulling their faces out of the water every few feet to sputter and breathe.

Troy, head lifeguard, full-time burnout, and serious heartbreaker, watches them intently, the edge of his clipboard balanced on his tight stomach. He squats down, encouraging and coaxing them along as he checks that no toes are touching the bottom of the pool. If they can make it across, from ladder to ladder without touching, they pass the test and can swim alone in the shallow end, no grown-up necessary.

My first shift of the summer is at the far end of the L-shaped pool, to the left of the aqua-colored diving boards, where the water is twelve feet deep and everyone wants to hang out.

I am joined by Troy's blond band of brothers. All the other lifeguards, minus one, are junior Troys in training. Just like Troy, but younger, blonder, and browner, they are the future insurance salesmen of our fair town, with one exception. Margo, the only other girl, if you can call her that, is squat and thick and has the lats my parents feared. Her voice is like a trombone with the slide all the way out.

The hot slab of cement surrounding the three sides of the diving well is the place to be. It is far enough away from the pool office for a little privacy, yet close enough to the parking lot for boys to flirt from the far side of the fence and friends without season passes to drop by and catch up on the latest.

I tap my feet against the long legs of my tall chair and twirl my whistle around my fingers, eager to fall into my summer routine. At least one swimmer in the well would be nice.

I check the road over my right shoulder. No cars. The baseball fields, empty. Straining my eyes behind the cover of my dark sunglasses, I try to see all the way down to the bottom of the hill. It's been only a couple of hours, but I'm jonesing to see him again.

A flapping beach towel catches my eye. A lone sunbather is shaking out her towel and setting up camp across the water from me. I take in the pale skin and thin limbs as they settle onto a shabby striped beach towel from the only place around here that rents rooms by the hour, Towne's Tiki Motel. Good god, Valerie Dickens is at the pool.

She is reading *Moby Dick* poolside, with no apparent irony. Her skinny arms look as if they have never seen the sun and can barely hold up the hardcover. She rests the book on her concave stomach to turn the page.

She is definitely preparing for an academic showdown next year. Has to be. Why else would she feel the need to read an American classic in my presence? She has never been to the pool before. I'm not even sure she can swim.

I grab the Coke I planted in the shade under my seat at the beginning of my shift and swallow a huge gulp. I try to ignore Valerie. I watch for green cars instead.

"Leah."

I jump as a hand touches my ankle. Troy laughs.

"You missed the whistle," he says, tapping his fingers on my toes. "Time to move."

My feet sizzle on the cement as I make my way through a parting sea of preteen girls to the next lifeguard chair. I can feel them watching me, looking me up and down, as I turn the first corner at the base of the high dive. I smooth my ponytail over my shoulder and look straight back at them. The braver ones smile at me, the others look away quickly, as if I didn't notice that they were just totally staring at me. You'd think I would be used to it by now. If I were Yorke, I would smile and give them all a twirl or, at the very least, the finger.

Turning the second corner, the one by the low dive, I pause for a second, squinting through the golden hue my sunglasses cast on the world as a car slows in the lot, the driver waving in my general direction. But it is only a bright blue Mini. I don't wave back, and the Mini rolls right on by as I look away and find myself caught in Valerie Dickens's evil stare.

"Rest assured you are enjoying your summer, Leah," she says, leaning on a razor-sharp elbow to drop one of those old lady bookmarks complete with a yarn tassel into *Moby Dick*'s yawning crack. Her sarcasm is not lost on me. It is as thick as Mr. Hobart's stubby fingers.

I walk slowly past her, smirking at the stack of library books tumbling from her beach bag and the sunburn on her nose. The page beneath her is dripping in neon, almost every line highlighted. Who brings a highlighter to the pool? I should let her drown.

"Let me give you a sneak peak," I say, lifting my sunglasses and smiling my sweetest smile as I lean in close to her.

"The captain dies," I whisper, and the highlighter goes slack in her hand. I climb up onto my chair, flick my hair over my shoulder, and blow my whistle extra loud at nothing in particular.

Five

"Leah," my mother says, finally having taken her seat at the head of the table with an approving nod, apparently feeling no need to fuss any further with the placement of the napkins and glasses and the forks, "please pass the peas."

Then, looking to where my dad is still messing about at the barbecue, a platter of grilled chicken in his hand and the sun sinking low in the sky behind him, she asks, "Mason, are you about ready over there?"

Turning back to the table, she smooths her napkin as she places it on her lap and announces loud enough for my dad to hear over the sputtering flames of the grill, "We are going shopping for wedding dresses tomorrow afternoon."

The clang of the barbecue tongs is followed by the quick shuffle of my dad's house slippers across the patio.

"Here it is," he says, setting an oval platter in the middle of the table. "I was just burning one for Freddie."

We are sitting at our old teak table on the patio near the deep end of our pool. The table is one of the few things that made the move from the old lake house, my mother insisting everything else be brand-new in her brand-new house.

I miss our old house. I miss the trees. I miss the lake. I even miss being crammed into the tiny kitchen with the teapot wallpaper, the talk of books and boys and sweaters borrowed without permission looping around the worn round table at dinnertime. Our tight connection seems to have dissolved somehow into the extra square footage and vaulted ceilings of this new place. It may be twice the size, but it's half as much like home.

"When are you getting married?" Freddie asks, her index finger slipping down the last page of the book in her lap.

Curious about why she is reading on the sly, I lean back and read the title, *France: Rough and Ready*. No wonder. I don't think my mother is in favor of any of us roughing anything, anywhere, at any time.

Yorke is sipping her iced tea. Her glass is so full ice is rushing the rim, threatening to go overboard.

"The end of the summer." My mother answers for her, starting the bowl of potatoes on their one-way trip around the table.

Yorke swallows quickly and confirms with a nod. "End of the summer."

I scoop some mashed potatoes onto my plate and set the heavy bowl down next to my dad's elbow.

"So soon?" I ask, turning the spoon toward him.

"We have to . . ." Yorke says as she pauses to examine each piece of chicken on the platter before reaching over and dropping a severely burned one on Freddie's plate and a less burned one on her own.

"You know," she continues, licking her fingers, "before Freddie leaves for France."

She hands the platter to me. All the good burned ones are gone.

"Freddie is my maid of honor after all," Yorke says. "So she needs to be there."

"Do I need to be there?" I ask, stabbing at a piece of chicken.

Feeling my mother's eyes boring into me, I realize my blunder and recover quickly.

"I mean, for the shopping," I say, and add clearly, "not the wedding."

"Of course you need to be there," my mother says.

Yorke drops her fork onto her plate with a loud clink and flops back into her chair dramatically.

"When you get engaged," my mother continues, "Yorke and Freddie will be more than happy to shop with you."

Whoa, I think, one sister at a time, please.

I bet she has little cake toppers already made for all of us. She probably ordered them in bulk. A little porcelain me in a pink dress and a little porcelain man in a white suit and pink bow tie are waiting for the big day, wrapped in tissue paper and stowed away in the hope chest at the foot of her bed.

"It's just that I have to work," I say, looking over at Yorke's unsympathetic face.

"Can't you just take the day off or switch with somebody or something?" she asks, circling her fork in the air. For her, it's as easy as pie. Believe it or not, Yorke has never had a job. Go figure.

"That job," my mother huffs as she pours more chardonnay into her half-full glass, "is more trouble than it is worth."

It's only one short week into summer, and she is already bitching about my job.

Setting the bottle down a little too hard, she asks me, though I know it is meant for my dad, too, "I thought we agreed that you would work early in the day at the pool so that we could still enjoy our summers as a family?"

Next to me, Freddie is sawing away at her black chicken with a thick wooden-handled steak knife. If I didn't know her, I would think she wasn't paying attention at all. But I know Freddie. She is always listening.

"What time are you shopping?" my dad asks, sliding the chardonnay bottle out of my mother's reach.

"Four," Yorke says. She leans back and crosses her arms, ready for a confrontation.

"And what time do you have to be at the pool?" my dad asks me, his eyes saying, Help me out here, Leah.

"Six-thirty."

"Well, there you go," my dad says with a smile, proud of his ability to take a situation and simplify it. Such a dude. He picks up his fork. "Plenty of time," he says. "Problem solved."

But nothing is that simple for my mother. You would think my dad, of all people, would know that by now.

She purses her lips and adjusts the placement of her wineglass before she complicates things by saying, "Except that Leah will have to leave early to walk to the pool." She lifts her glass and drains the chardonnay in one golden gulp.

"Or," she continues, "one of us will have to leave early to drive her there. Either way," she says with a shake of her head, "it hardly seems worth it."

"Maybe she could drive herself?" Freddie says, breaking her vow of silence with a most useless contribution.

I give her a woeful stare.

"For once." Yorke agrees emphatically. "I don't know why you bought her that car anyway."

"You got a car," my mother says.

"Yeah, that I *drive*," says Yorke.

My dad holds up his hands.

"Leah will drive her car when she wants to," he says calmly.

Doubtful, but I do appreciate his support. My mother reaches past Yorke for the bottle of wine and refills her glass. Afraid she is just adding more fuel to the fire, I raise my hands and admit defeat.

"I'll get Shane," I say, looking around the table

to be sure everyone understands the terms of my surrender. "Shane will drive me."

"What about his two-a-days?" my dad asks, needing to be sure that all bases are covered before he signs off on this plan.

"They're done by then," Freddie says.

I know that Freddie knows the summer practice schedule because Evan played football even though he was only the kicker, but I think she is really just trying to make up for her car comment.

"Okay then," my dad says, rubbing his hands together briskly and giving a little clap. He seems pleased. "Okay?" he asks, looking at each one of us expectantly.

"Okay." Yorke agrees with a nod.

Freddie nods, too, but we know it all hangs on my mother.

She agrees reluctantly, pointing her fork at me, punctuating each word. "Tomorrow. Four o'clock. Sharp," she says.

I nod. It seems that this meal, like everything else in my life, starts and ends with her approval.

♥ ♥ ♥

Yorke is looking for something princessy with an empire waist. "Not too ornate, but definitely with beading," she says, lifting the silk skirt of a sample dress limply between her fingers. "And white. Definitely white," she adds. The bridal shop ladies scatter in every direction, hell-bent on being the one to find the perfect dress for the perfect bride, and make the commission, too.

My mother and I are sitting on a cream-colored chintz love seat kind of thing with a bony, curved spine made of wood that presses into your back right where you want to lean in and get comfortable.

The entire bridal shop is white, ivory, and cream. The walls are covered in a white-on-white flowered fabric, or maybe it's velvet wallpaper, if there is such a thing.

There are no sharp edges or harsh angles, everything is curved or soft or poufed. An ornate coffee table, loaded with lilies and every other kind of white flower imaginable, sits between us and the dresses that Freddie and Yorke are flicking through indiscriminately.

"Explain to me please, Leah," my mother says, smoothing her hand lightly across my back and lowering her voice, "why you are wearing a bathing suit under your dress?"

She fingers the lump between my shoulder blades where I twisted the straps of my red suit together with an elastic band to make it shorter, less boy cut, and more user-friendly.

"I don't like to change at the pool," I say, sliding out from under her grasp and developing a sudden interest in wedding dresses. "All those girls stare."

"Get used to it," Freddie says, her head poking out of a slinky, long, super-low-cut satin dress.

"Why aren't you used to it?" Yorke asks.

She is standing on a raised dais that is covered in thick creamy shag and sits in front of three gilded full-length mirrors. She rotates slowly, checking her reflection in each mirror before she looks at me.

"You do have a lot to stare at," she says.

Freddie laughs from somewhere behind yards of

tulle, and Yorke turns back to the mirrors. I look at her double A chest reflecting back at me. Even in triplicate it still doesn't amount to much.

"I'm not trying on dresses today anyway," I say. "You are."

"But if we find a bridesmaid dress that I like, you'll need to try it on," Yorke says, her eyes searching the mirrors for my mother. They nod together.

"Freddie can do it," I say, inspecting the lace on a hideously ugly dress with a hoop skirt and some kind of boning inside. "You can just pretend it's me, but, you know, without any boobs." I grin.

Freddie drops the dress she is holding and stalks past me.

"Besides," I say to Yorke, watching the assistants marching down the hall toward us, their arms laden with white gowns zippered away in clear plastic bags, "it is going to take you a hundred years to find your dress."

Freddie turns to me. "She doesn't have a hundred years," she says.

"Girls, girls." My mother shushes us in a low

voice. She clears her throat and sits up straight on the little love seat, tucking her feet primly underneath her. She angles her head toward the arriving assistants and smiles. "The dresses are here."

It's sad but true—Yorke must buy off the rack. Her wedding date is too soon for anything custom made. I settle in and watch my mother and Yorke slowly coming to terms with the true meaning of these words and then lean back, ready for the show.

Yorke steps onto the pedestal, wearing the first off-the-rack option, her politely disguised look of disgust reflecting back at us from every angle.

"Oh, Yorke." My mother gasps, turning away from the dress in horror. Lifting her hand to shield her eyes, she says, "That one is too . . . *Gone with the Wind*."

It does have incredibly big shoulders. My mother dismisses Yorke, and the dress, with a brisk wave of her hand, and Yorke disappears into the dressing room to try again.

Freddie takes Yorke's place on the pedestal, forced by my mother to try something on since all gown-related decisions have been switched into high gear. She steps up in front of the three mirrors, slumping her shoulders and taking my breath away.

I know what my crime was. I was found guilty of wearing a bathing suit as an undergarment to a dress fitting and am serving my time here, sitting next to my mother on the smallest of sofas. I am not certain of Freddie's offense, but the punishment is clear. She is wearing the ugliest tangerine satin dress ever, with a low-slung bow at the waist and satin pumps, dyed to match.

Choking on my tea, I manage to say, "All you need is a corsage of carnations and baby's breath."

My mother raises her arched brows at me and lifts her teacup to take a sip. There is only one coral lip print on the rim. She hits it exactly, every time.

"You look like a prom reject from 1982," Yorke says as she sweeps back into the room wearing a tight white mermaid gown, pulling a long train behind her. "Take it off."

"Jinny has that particular dress available in a variety of colors," my mother explains, smiling at Jinny, the shop owner with the bouffant black hair, who is discreetly orchestrating her assistants from the edge of the room.

My mother clasps her hands together and suggests, wistfully, "Leah could wear it in pink, and Freddie could wear it in yellow."

Freddie is a citrus blur against the velvety white walls as she spins toward my mother, shouting, "No!"

"Mother," Yorke snaps, as she steps up onto the dais, "no!"

Knowing that I am most likely prolonging my time in the chintz-covered penalty box, I look over at Jinny and ask, sweetly, "Does that particular dress come in a light blue?"

Her assistants are ready to scramble, eager to break the tension that is rising in the showroom, happy to find a blue dress or any dress at all.

My mother shakes her head at Jinny, admitting defeat, calling off the color-coded wedding and the assistants without a word. She wraps her fingers around my leg and presses down, squeezing. "Yorke will be wearing something borrowed, and something blue, and a beautiful *white* gown," she explains to the room as if Yorke, preening around in front of the mirrors in the tightest wedding dress ever made, her nonexistent chest squeezed right up and almost out of the top to touch her chin, were the epitome of the vestal virgin bride.

"But not that one." My mother sighs loudly. "It's too tight," she says. She lays her hands lightly across her girdle-wrapped middle. "I can practically see your lunch."

One pot of Earl Grey and fifteen white dresses later, we are still searching for "the one." Well, really, my mother and Yorke and Freddie are searching. I am staring out the front window of the bridal shop, sipping my tea and watching the street for a car to pull up and take me away. The room is full of hot air and high tea, and I am steeped.

I see Shane driving up the street toward us, right on time for once.

The sun gleams off his chrome vanity plate as SHN ROX swings out wide, comes in fast, and angles against the curb. He checks himself in the rearview mirror, flicking his bangs to the right before he steps out of the car and into the perfumed bridal shop. The clatter of the bells hanging over the door and the rush of the bracelets down my mother's arm announce his arrival.

"Well, there he is." My mother laughs, stretching out her arms to greet him.

"Any luck?" Shane asks as he leans down to receive my mother's kiss.

Yorke strides out of the dressing room, toes lost in the thick cream carpet, wearing nothing but a strapless bra under a loosely tied short satin robe.

"Nope," she says.

Shane's eyes bulge out of their sockets as her robe slips open when she slides down onto the love seat, shoving me over and squeezing me out.

"I'm ready," I say abruptly, standing and blocking Shane's view.

"And Fred?" Shane asks hopefully, his eyes searching the room.

I point to her feet, just visible under the curved door of a dressing room.

Shane stares at the door, his dreams dashed. I guess he was hoping for three Johnson sisters in a state of undress today. He is totally pissing me off, so he will be lucky if he makes it to two.

"So, we're good to go?" Shane asks, looking past me and doing the standard double check with my mother before he reaches down to grab my bag.

"You can take her away," my mother replies. "We are done with her."

Sliding into Shane's car is the same as diving into a pool of warm water on a hot day. It feels thick, soupy, and unsettling. He shifts into drive and automatically drops his hand onto my leg. I lean my head back and close my eyes tight against that heavy feeling, but it glows burning and red against my lids, no matter how hard I try to shut it out.

❤ ❤ ❤

I stand with my knees locked, my bare legs pressing against the metal seat behind me, my eyes on the grade schoolers.

Having spent the afternoon navigating the crowded, choppy waters of the pool, they now hang limply from the chain-link fence while the sun sets over their freckled shoulders. They look wrung out. I can relate.

Balancing on their rusty three-speeders in damp bathing suits, they sit out the hour while the pool is closed between the afternoon and night swims. They live here all summer, like refugees. It's not just a pool; it's a baby-sitting service with free chlorine.

Finally Troy climbs onto his chair, and bicycles drop to the ground like flies. The refugees are ready, good for another go. I, however, am not so sure I have it in me.

When the sharp sound of Troy's whistle finally splits the soft evening air, I buckle. I pull my legs in close to my body and lean back, with nothing more to do than watch little kids and their parents paddle around for the next two hours while the sun goes down and the temperature sinks.

The greased-up girls of the afternoon, lying side by side on thick beach towels with their bikini straps lowered, are gone. The guys in dark denim and worn baseball caps who sweat in the sun as they flirt and chat with the sunbathers have long since disappeared. They hopped into their cars for a smoke before heading off for a night at the lake.

Tonight it's mostly families, little kids and parents who have put on a few pounds since their dating days. They do this thing—I remember it from last summer—where they take the first few embarrassing steps, the ones after they drop the beach towel but before they hit the water, on their tiptoes. Like that makes them look skinnier or something.

A breeze lifts the branches that dangle over the top of the fence, and I take a deep breath. It feels like the first one of the day.

Lights are popping up all over the park. Bright circles of white light suddenly appear over splintery teeter-totters, dusty home plates, and empty grass lots, making the night seem instantly darker, the sky more indigo.

The overhead lights around the perimeter of the pool buzz and flicker to life just as Valerie Dickens steps out of the changing room, momentarily caught, all pink and bookish, in her very own fluorescent spotlight.

After yesterday's outing I thought she would need to stay in the shade and administer cold drinks. Instead she's back, and she's wearing some kind of shiny Ravi Shankar caftan that sways around her ankles as she slowly makes her way from the changing room to my side of the pool.

Freddie went through this totally annoying Beatles phase, so I know who Ravi Shankar is. Freddie and Evan would sit in her room with a lava lamp on and listen to *Yellow Submarine* over and over and over. Yorke told her it was worth it only if she was going to get high, or at least listen to *Sgt. Pepper's*, but at the time Freddie was not willing to risk any brain cells or her chance at being valedictorian.

I'll bet that is what next year is for—illicit drugs and sex abroad. Although I know Freddie and Evan already do it. I guess he talked about it in the locker room after practice, so everybody knows, but the idea totally grosses me out.

I just don't think Evan is cute, although that really doesn't make sense since he is just a lankier version of Shane, who is just a younger version of Evan, who kind of looks like my dad, and Roger looks like them all but just a bit more pinched and trimmed. *Merde.*

Valerie walks by my chair, a scuffed and scraped canvas tote bag heavy with books slung over one bony shoulder and the edge of her striped beach towel swiping along behind her on the deck. I can't resist.

I lean down, smiling fakely, my Lycra-covered boobs pressing warmly onto the tops of my knees as I ask, "Can I expect this pleasure every day?"

"I bought a season pass," she replies, slowing for a moment to grin back at me with a smile just as fake as mine, before she continues on, pulling at her beach towel in an ongoing struggle to drag it up onto her book-free shoulder and walk at the same time.

Watching her go, the towel trailing over her shoulder like a terry-cloth boa, I lean back and think, Well, there goes her science fair money.

Troy clicks on the office radio, and classic rock rolls across the surface of the pool, filling the spaces between the lazy splashes and soft laughter and the occasional odd remark from Valerie.

"That man is absolutely rotund," she says suddenly, to no one apparently, and I look over to see her examining a fat man waddling across the deck near the shallow end in a disturbingly tight madras suit.

I can practically hear her bones grinding against the cement from way up here when she rolls onto her stomach, pulls a pink highlighter from between her front teeth, and watches a diver arc off the high dive.

"Not a good angle," she comments like an Olympic judge, lowering her eyes back down to her book.

The diver is still underwater, making his way through the glowing water of the diving well, so I am guessing the ongoing dialogue is meant for me.

When she calls out, "George Washington Carver was an excellent swimmer," I have no doubt. She is trying to lead me astray educationally and drive me bat shit at the same time.

I decide to ignore her completely. First because I don't think her views regarding the swimming skills of the preeminent inventor of peanut agricultural science are true or in any way verifiable, but mostly because I think it should cost anyone, and especially her, way more than fifty-five dollars to get to torture me for the entire summer.

At the stroke of nine, mostly everybody packs up and heads for the exits, weary and wet—everyone except for Valerie.

She is attempting to wedge an entire library full of books, probably according to the Dewey decimal system, back into her bag and is temporarily rendered speechless by the effort.

I am cleaning my side of the pool, stretching out

as far as I can to reach the middle with the long-handled skimmer, straining for a bug or a Band-Aid or something that is floating just beyond my reach, when, from right behind me, Valerie asks, "So . . . Shane got a new car?"

I jump and sink the bug or whatever it is to the murky depths. I look over my shoulder, struggling to see past the bright headlights as a car pulls right up onto the grassy slope next to the pool.

It is a big, black, shiny SUV, the kind with dark-tinted windows and those fancy rims that spin. I move toward the fence, dragging the skimmer behind me.

The lights flash once. Twice. Off. I reach up to put the skimmer away, squinting into the deep darkness, and catch my finger in the skimmer latch. I inhale sharp and fast.

"That's not Shane," I breathe as the driver's door cracks open.

"Hey, lifeguard."

He walks toward the pool, hair messy, a blue T-shirt that says RAY'S MIDTOWN CYCLES half tucked into faded jeans that are held up by a thick worn belt. His belt tweaks up at the end with a little leather curl instead of behaving and lying flat.

"Hey, Porter."

He looks me up and down as he hooks his fingers into the fence just above his left shoulder and then says, "Nice whistle."

My pulse starts to race. I am vibrating. Like the little summer bugs circling the lamps above our heads, I know I am about to get burned, but I am still kind of looking forward to the sizzle.

"Thanks," I manage as the sound of a heavy canvas bag being hoisted onto a razor-sharp shoulder stops the buzzing in my brain and brings my attention back to Valerie.

I try to ignore her, but I can feel her gaze burning into my back as she walks away, measuring, dissecting, parsing, syllabicating.

Troy clicks the underwater lights off, and the smooth pool water goes dramatically dark.

Porter leans away from the fence and stuffs his hands into his pockets.

"Are you done here?" he asks.

"I guess," I say with a shrug.

I can hear Troy behind me, digging around on the desk, swearing and shuffling newspapers and sign-in sheets with his burly man hands, searching for his keys, the way he does at the end of every night swim, so he can lock up.

"Okay," Porter says, and I don't know what that means.

Is it like, Okay, I'll see you later, or Okay, I'll wait, or Okay, I gotta go, 'cause my girlfriend is waiting in the car?

"Okay," I say.

His smile slides open, and I feel his eyes following me as I walk away, my bare feet padding softly on the cement. I am glad that I am wearing this suit, glad that I can fill it out, and glad that I am not wearing a caftan and carrying a prehistoric book bag like Valerie.

She is eyeballing me from the path outside the pool as I leave through the side gate. I wave to Troy as he clicks off the office light, pulls the door shut behind him, and then turns to put his key in the lock.

Porter is sitting on top of a graffiti-carved picnic table, his beat-up work boots on the bench, elbows propped on his knees, watching me make my way across the grassy slope. Valerie's car rattles behind me as she drives off.

As I get closer, he rises slowly, stretches, and slides his hands down his thighs before standing tall. I pause, my flip-flops flipping to a stop as he walks back over to the black SUV.

"Just how many cars do you have?" I ask, stalling against his presumption that I will just hop into the car with him and my eagerness to do just that.

"Me?" He gives the chrome handle of the driver's door a smooth tug.

The SUV is highly polished, so clean that under the amber hum of the streetlights I can see the tree branches overhead reflecting back at me from the shiny hood.

"Zero."

In my head I tally the cars I have seen him

driving as he slides up onto the high leather seat. I can count three at least.

"You want a ride?" he asks, a tan work boot dangling casually over the edge of the silver-and-black running board.

My brain is working away. *Zero cars*? Wait. Does that first red car I saw him in count? Because technically, the red car was borrowed from Roger, if you don't use the strict definition of *borrowed*, so my total is two. Right?

Porter flips the SUV key over and over in the palm of his hand. His leg still dangles from the open door.

"I don't know," I say, unsure.

"Okay." He nods and pulls the door shut with a deliberate and expensive-sounding thump.

I take a few steps toward the car, slowly and cautiously. He puts the key in the ignition and starts it up.

Resting his arm along the edge of the open window, he looks out at the pool, then past the fence to the dark, deserted park. His green eyes are questioning and unsure when they settle on mine.

"You sure?" he asks.

I shrug and look down, twisting my toe into the thick grass, as I wait for him to ask again, expecting him to talk me into it the way Shane or any other boy would. Instead he drops the car into reverse, slides his arm along the back of the passenger seat as he twists to check behind him, and leaves me just standing there with my mouth open while he rolls away.

In that small second between reverse and drive—you know, that little lull after you stop backing up but before the car actually starts moving forward, while the machinery is working and the gears are turning or whatever—in that second he turns and looks over at me standing alone on the grassy rise, gaping. He waves, rests his hand on the wheel, and guns it.

My bag slips from my shoulder, and I wave back five seconds too late. I thought he would beg a little bit. I curl my toes tight into my flip-flops and bounce down the hill, not breathing, not thinking, gripping against the dewy grass and hoping I am not too late.

"Porter!" I yell into the spray of gravel landing at my feet as the wheels hit the edge of the road. I jog a couple of steps into the middle of the street and stop to shout at the back of the SUV again. "Porter!"

The silvery rims spin backward as he slows to a stop. He adjusts the rearview mirror and looks back at me like, what the hell? But at least he stops.

I take the few strides between me and the SUV at a clumsy tear and tap on the tinted glass of the passenger door, out of breath and full of embarrassment. Porter leans across the seat and opens the door with a wry smile.

I smooth my ponytail back with buzzing hands and a pumping pulse, because I don't want him to think I am hard up or anything, and try to compose myself as I climb in.

Warm lake air spills in through the open windows, mixing into a sweaty storm of lips and breath, stirring the interior of the parked SUV as I curse the inventor of the one-piece swimsuit. Porter's hands are sliding up the slippery Lycra fabric of my regulation lifeguard suit while I straddle him in the front seat.

Cottages dot the shore on the far side of the lake; the yellow glow of porch lights and the stars sprinkling the sky illuminate his quick, skillful movements.

"What the hell," Porter says as he snaps a thick red strap. "How do I get into this thing?" He slides his hands up my back. "It's like a chastity suit."

I laugh as I lean forward to kiss him. "My father would be so proud."

"Mine, too," he says.

I lean back with the realization that other than this sudden mention of family, I know absolutely nothing about this guy. Except that he is a very fast driver, always wears boots, smells like beach and forest somehow mixed together with mint, and has the most dangerous green eyes.

I know he can drive and kiss at the same time (but we only did that for a little while), can get my shirt off in five seconds flat, yet is confounded by a tight red bathing suit.

He doesn't talk a lot. Will leave a girl screaming in the street. Doesn't push me farther than I want to go but takes me right to the edge and somehow makes me want more. But how does he know what I want? How does he know me at all?

"Why am I here right now?" I ask abruptly, feeling the steering wheel against my back as I lean away from him.

He returns my look directly as his thumbs circle lightly on my bare shoulders. "Hey," he says, his eyes softening, sparkling even in the dark car, "you chased me down. Remember?"

"Oh, right," I say, and I dive in, losing myself again in the warm pulse at the base of his neck. I did.

My parents are secreted away in our cozy family room when I finally arrive home, late and looking downright manhandled. A sneak peek in the mirror by our front door reveals that my hair is loose and wild, tumbling over my shoulders. My lips are raw and bare. I am not even wearing a shirt over my suit.

My mother is curled up in the corner of the sofa, her small feet tucked under my dad's splayed legs. His head is back, and a light snore rumbles from his slack mouth as a movie plays on the large screen across the room, the sound turned down low and quiet.

"Shane couldn't come in?" my mother asks without looking up. The harsh light from the TV flickers across her face, actually making her look her age for once.

"Nope," I say from the arched doorway, bare feet on the cool tile, pausing long enough for her to turn and look at me, and wondering, when she doesn't, what else I could have gotten up to that she wouldn't notice.

I head for the stairs, feeling a bit robbed, as if I had put in all these years of fending off Shane for nothing since she couldn't even be bothered to notice when I managed to stray. I never really understood why everyone, Yorke especially, was so into boys and always sneaking away in the night and making out. I get it now.

Pulling myself up the polished staircase railing toward my room, I make a vow never to wear this red suit again, at least not as underwear, even though I am certain that tonight my virtue was saved by its impenetrable skintight Lycra.

Who knows what could have happened without it? I shiver to think. I could have been seriously plundered, taken to places Shane has never even thought of. Long live the maillot, as Freddie would say, but I feel a little let down and a little bit trapped by the typical end to this rare Saturday night, so I vow, safe and sound inside my own house, never again to mistake a bathing suit for an undergarment. That, and I will always wear lip gloss. I can guarantee, the lip gloss my mother will notice.

There are voices coming from Freddie's room. I assume it is Freddie and her French friend Gérard, rolling through some late-night French phrasing. But no, the intonation is off, and there is a lot more mumbling and whispering than you would expect from a language lesson.

Yorke is lying on Freddie's bed. She's wearing a tiny UofW T-shirt and striped underwear, combing through her hair with her fingers, inspecting any split end she comes across under the dim glow of the shawl-covered lamp at the head of the bed.

Freddie is there, too, facing the other direction, flat on her back with a thick paperback resting on her stomach.

Stopping in the dark hall, just outside the pink pall cast by Freddie's lamp, I wonder what happened tonight to lead them here, head to toe and toe to head, all sisterly and snuggly.

At the old lake house, in the blue-wallpapered room they shared, the best games and tea parties and secret ceremonies always seemed to take place on the round braided rug. Without me. I remember them walking off hand in hand in matching ankle socks to summer camp, while I stayed at home in my ankle socks with my mother, consoled by a new doll that had a tiny backpack full of miniature camping supplies.

Or later, their golden hair long and loose, when they both moved past braids and barrettes and into high school, leaving me alone and adrift in the pimply world of eighth grade. My dad always says that girls work better in threes. I think three always leaves one left out.

Freddie looks over at me. Yorke notices Freddie and stops talking mid-sentence. Yorke gives me a cool look, as if I had stumbled onto something private and secret. I instantly feel about six years old.

Freddie rolls over onto her side and flips up on one elbow.

"Shane called," she says.

Digging to the bottom of my bag, I find and check my phone. Two texts. That's Dani and Len, for sure. And four missed calls. Shit.

"The house, too?" I ask.

Freddie looks over at Yorke for confirmation.

"Yep." She nods.

She gives me another look before she rolls onto her back and crosses one long leg over the other, her foot bouncing impatiently as she picks up her book.

Yorke sighs and piles her hair on the top of her head in a sloppy twist.

"In case you are wondering," she says, sounding very put out as she crosses her arms and snuggles the tiny T-shirt tight against her just as tiny chest, "I told Shane you were out with the girls."

Girls? What girls? Truth be told, I don't really have that many friends, and my sisters know it. Just Dani and Len. For the past couple of years it's been Dani on my left and Len on my right, a descending line in order of height, in AP classes, pep practice, and at lunch. Even in the hallways. You'd think I would miss them, considering that they are gone for the summer, but I haven't considered them much at all.

My sisters' eyes flick over at me, presuming and slightly eager, watching my face. They are ready to hear my story, my excuse for disappearing for a couple of hours, ignoring my phone and my family and my boyfriend.

I know what they want. They want me to tell them everything, the way I always have, so they can compare and contrast my actual behavior with what it should have been, what it always has been. I take a deep breath and prepare to have my brain picked clean.

I exhale and say nothing. I am not ready to have every detail of tonight exposed and examined and faded. Or bleached like bones in the sun. I walk away, leaving them waiting, knitted together in the pink glow of Freddie's room. I know I will pay for this escape later. But for now all I want is to keep this part of my life mine.

"You're welcome," Yorke yells, all peeved and huffy, as I disappear down the dark hall.

I open the window over my bed, welcoming the damp smell of summer into my over-air-conditioned room as I climb into bed. I don't bother to listen to my messages. Or even take off my bathing suit. I pull my duvet up over my head and slip off into sleep.

Six

The park is steamy and silent, the grass along the side of the road still sleeping under a thick blanket of dew. The solid plank picnic tables and industrial green picnic shelters are slick with condensation that will dry as the sun creeps up.

An engine rumbles at my heels, the sound of loose pea gravel under heavy tires popping in my ears as my interest in my feet and their ability to take one step in front of the other becomes unprecedented.

How stupid am I to think that he would show up every day? Any day? I'm sure he's got other stuff to do, girls to see, cars to drive. Whatever it is that he does with his life that I don't know about. Like everything.

But how do I get my heart to stop skipping a beat whenever I hear a car coming my way? I don't know. All I know is after almost a week I feel as if I am slowly rolling backward, like there will be no more surprises in my life, ever. I know the next move I am supposed to make, and the next and the next.

Just follow Yorke and Freddie, pass go, and collect my two hundred dollars. But what I really want to do is turn that little silver car around and squeal away, running over the shoe and the Scottie dog and knocking over the tiny plastic hotels and houses as I go.

I take a couple of slow staring-at-the-ground steps, switching my bag from one shoulder to the other with the tiniest flick of my head, catching only the polished chrome of a bumper out of the corner of my eye.

Keeping my head down, I pretend I am walking across a low balance beam just like I did in kindergarten—heel to toe, heel to toe. But God, I already know it's him. I knew it as soon as I felt the engine rumbling down the street, vibrating through the soles of my flip-flops, thrumming right into my chest, then sparking out the tips of my fingers.

Besides, who would drive up so close and so slow? With no hello, no honk of the horn, no warning at all? Nobody but Porter, that's who.

"Is this becoming a habit?" he asks.

You have no idea, I think as I turn, twisting toward him on my toes in the deep loose gravel.

He is about two feet behind me, parked wildly across the middle of the one-way street, manning a serious muscle car and blocking anyone's chance to make an early-morning dash down the hill. Sparkly and midnight blue, the car's got two thick black racing stripes on the hood and a fancy black line that streams along the sides before ending in a scripted curl by the back tires. All the chrome is polished into a dimension beyond shiny.

It's the kind of car you never see in real life, not driving down the street anyway. You see cars like this only in calendars that hang in the auto shop where my dad takes his truck for service or in the stinky junk-filled lockers of gearheads at school. It looks as if it is just waiting for a bikini model to drape herself across the hood, arch her back, and smile for the camera.

"How about an addiction?" I blurt, and then I freeze, feeling transparent. My eagerness and interest in him are as easy to read as the well-polished hood ornament staring back at me. All silver and shiny, it says desperate, I mean Dodge.

"Either way," he says, dropping his hand down to rest on the outside of the driver's door as he looks at me with raised eyebrows, "you might need professional help."

When he smiles that smile at me that lights up his whole face, I feel alert, buzzing. Crap. It appears my lust has no clock. That smile has the same effect on me at dawn as it does at dusk.

"Working today?" he asks.

A mower roars to life near the tree line as a jumpsuited boy working for the city begins the big, looping circles necessary to temporarily tame the thick shag that covers the park.

I struggle with my answer, weighing my desire not to look desperate against my desperation to see him again.

"Nope," I reply, the mental scales obviously tipping in his favor.

He looks down questioningly at the bag resting at my feet.

"Well," I say, smiling sheepishly, "not till later."

I look away, feeling embarrassed, and move my hands around in the general direction of the pool. I know I have a serious Porter problem. I would like to provide evidence to the contrary, but really, here I am at the crack of dawn, lips all glossy, goodies encased in pink lace, my bathing suit packed neatly in my bag with my whistle. And I don't even have to work this morning.

"Then what are you doing here?" he asks.

My brain thinks, Duh, waiting for you, but

somehow I manage to keep my lips closed as I twist my fingers in my hair and tilt my head. My brain goes from zero to sixty, trying to skirt the obvious. I'm like that science experiment we learned about in eighth grade with the bell and the dogs, no matter how much I loathe the comparison. The sound of a car engine now equals my head turning. I can't even imagine what would happen if someone flashed headlights at me. I would probably run barefoot down a street paved in glass.

Avoiding his gaze, I settle for "You know, not much."

I know I am a crappy liar. You'd think I would have learned a little from living with the master, but while Yorke can spin lies of evangelical proportion, I never really got the hang of it. I fumble, I dither, I make an ass of myself and lose track of what I've said or thought and then go back and botch it up again. Not good. Now I steal a page from Freddie's book and keep quiet, letting my lame explanation soak in.

The classic leather upholstery squeaks slightly

under his jeans as Porter leans over and pulls up the lock on the passenger door. He smiles at me again and gives the heavy door a big push, swinging it open.

"Let's change that," he says.

I raise my eyebrows, my eyes asking yes, and his eyes are saying yes back, so I throw my bag into the tiny box of a backseat before he changes his mind and leaves me standing on the side of the road, again. At the very least I like to think I am learning.

I pull the door shut with a solid whump, and Porter snaps the radio on. The car is pristine inside, the stitched leather seats are smooth, and everything is polished and cared for.

Porter looks seriously out of place behind the leather steering wheel. His messy hair, wrinkled white T-shirt, and frayed jeans make me doubt this is his car.

The interior fills with the sounds of classic rock. I sit back and watch Porter drive, his wrist resting easily along the top of the wheel.

We pass the mowing boy. He has lowered his

jumpsuit, preparing for a hot day. It dangles as he swings around, the arms tied around his waist like a belt. He gives us a nod and a two-fingered wave before his loop swings him off in the opposite direction.

"Where are we going?" I ask over the engine and the radio and the mower.

Those green eyes flash at me for a second before he says, "For professional help." Then he reaches down, shifts smoothly, and guns the engine so hard that it drops me back into my seat.

When my parents were in high school, back before the spring dried up, when the water was still clear and cold, they used to come out here to the quarry to park and swim. Now it is just a graffiti-covered hole in the ground. Digging equipment is still parked at the bottom, rusted out and rotted. If I squint, it looks like a tiny scale model of the Grand Canyon, just way less colorful and much, much smaller.

Porter turns toward me, holds his hands up with his palms out, and tries to look like the picture of innocence as he says, "Let me start out by saying that I am not actually a professional."

"Okay."

"But I do think I can help you with your problem."

I sit back, slightly offended.

"I have a problem?"

He nods. "You know, they say the first step is admitting it."

God, I think, shrinking back and wrapping my arms tight across my chest, he knows I am addicted to him. Well, maybe it is obvious, but it's not like it warrants an intervention or anything.

"Let's switch," Porter says suddenly. He hops out of the car, leaving his door open while he runs around to my side.

Suddenly his white T is right there, at eye level outside my open window. He swirls his finger in the air impatiently.

"Switch!" he commands as he pulls my door open, and I barely have the time to step out before he drops into my seat and whips his finger around again, signaling me to go to the driver's side.

I crunch my way around the front of the car, watching Porter suspiciously out of the corner of my eye as I go. The sound of my door closing echoes across the empty quarry as I slide into Porter's seat. I reach up to adjust the rearview mirror. I check my hair.

I turn toward Porter and ask, "Sorry, but what exactly is my problem again?"

"One step at a time," he says calmly, and if I knew this guy better, at all really, I might think he was being condescending.

"First," he says as he reaches over, his hand wrapping warmly around my fingers, "let's get you comfortable handling the stick."

He lifts my hand, slowly pulls it toward him, and places it carefully onto the leather and chrome gearshift. He leaves his hand on top of mine for a second that simultaneously melts my fingers and my brain. He gives my fingers a tight squeeze and moves his hand away.

"Pistol grip," he says proudly with a tilt of his head toward the silver stick wrapped under my throbbing fingers.

"You're serious?" I ask incredulously, catching on to what he is after.

He nods at me with a smile.

"You know, I do have a license."

"Are you serious?" he asks, and his grin cracks open.

"Yes," I huff. "You want to see it?" I am already twisting, letting the prized pistol grip go as I reach into the tiny backseat for my bag.

Now, I don't know why it bothers him that I don't drive or why it bothers me that it bothers him. Other than my dad, who did buy me a brand-new car that just sits in our driveway, collecting dust and jealous glances from every teen in town, my lack of driving ability seems to bother no one at all. Well, maybe Yorke and my mother and probably Shane a little bit sometimes, too. But really, that's it.

I finally snag the padded strap of my backpack and pull the whole thing into my lap. I start digging around as Porter leans back, relaxing into that little space between the bucket seat and the passenger door.

Somewhere at the bottom of my bag, next to the whistle and some orphaned tampons, I find it, only slightly gobbed in a pool of melted lip balm. Legal, laminated proof that I can drive.

I hold it up for him to see, push it right into his doubting face, and say, "See?"

He takes it and studies it as if he can't believe it's real. He wipes it on his leg, leaving a cherry smear of lip stuff on his jeans, before he looks over at me.

"Nice picture," he says, tapping the plastic.

I snatch it back and drop it into the depths of my bag.

"Very funny," I mumble, feeling an unexpected flush rising on my cheeks.

I keep my head down, never meeting his eyes as I gather up the stuff that landed in my lap during my search. Keys, hairbrush, a bottle of dark blue nail polish that my mother banned from the house as soon as she saw my painted toes, assorted ponytail holders. I toss it all into my bag and throw my bag toward the backseat.

Porter sits still and quiet. The highway in the

distance, the road we took to get here, is the only sound I can hear over my short, heated breaths. Every other sound seems muted and swallowed up by the quarry in front of us.

It's as if Porter knew, somehow he knew, that if he just waited, I would get over this momentary bout of anger and bitchiness. That it is just temporary, 'cause I know he was joking, really only kidding, but I am nervous and scared, and I don't like to do things that I suck at. And I have a feeling that I am going to suck at this. Big time.

I breathe out. "Are we really doing this?" I ask.

"Just push in the clutch," he says.

Clutch? I am not really even sure where that would be. I look down toward my feet, hidden somewhere under the polished dashboard.

I wiggle my toes to prove to myself that they still exist and ask, "Can't I display my talents with, you know, a regular shifter?"

"An automatic?" he asks, and in that second I know he has lost all faith in me or at least in my professed driving ability.

I cautiously glance over and see him working his hand through his hair, ruffling it up.

"Let's see what you are really capable of," he says calmly as he smiles at me. "Then the rest will be easy."

I exhale again, loudly this time, blowing my hair out of my face as I turn toward him, my hands all tense and clammy, hoping that he will change his mind and somehow find his way back into the driver's seat, hoping that my nerves don't show on my face, but sure that they do.

"Just show me what you can do," he requests. "You told me yourself." He puts his hand over his heart as if he were reciting the pledge of allegiance and says in a crappy falsetto, "Your inability causes an aversion."

"For the record," I say, "I don't sound like that. And . . . " I continue as I reach down, fingers feeling gingerly along the edge of my seat with my left hand, "I need to be closer."

I fumble around for the lever to adjust things, but there is nothing there.

"In a real car," Porter says as he reaches over and leans close, his arm between my legs, "we keep it here."

I breathe him in as he finds the right part in exactly the right place, and I slide forward, while he leans back.

"Thanks," I say.

I like the seat nice and close so my arms can be at the required ten and two, with a slightly bent elbow and a firm grasp on the wheel. You know, just firm enough to make my knuckles white and shiny.

Porter raises his eyebrows. "It's common practice to drive with your arms and legs, not your boobs."

I am not a confident driver. I am not a confident driver who also happens to have big boobs, and I am sitting so close that they practically touch the steering wheel. Scoot me in a couple of inches, and they would push right through the steering wheel and wipe the classic dash clean.

"Hey," I say sharply to Porter without a glance in his general direction, "I passed my test this way."

"I bet you did," he agrees, and I look over to see

that his eyes are now locked on my chest.

It's weird to hear comments about your goods from someone who has actually touched them. I mean, I know he's touched them, I can remember it vividly, but it feels weird thinking about that when he is sitting right there, and I am sure he remembers he's touched them and he is probably remembering it right now, and maybe now is not the best time to be thinking about all this. I am about to drive after all.

I consider sliding the seat back a bit, but then I wouldn't be able to see clearly over the humongous striped hood to the rubble-filled death hole looming in front of us.

"I can drive, you know," I say, sliding my grip around on the slick wheel.

"You keep saying that," Porter replies, nodding toward the open lot around us. "Now let's see it."

I can't seem to get the hang of the clutch. Apparently it is a feeling, or at least that is what Porter keeps telling me, repeatedly, as we lurch forward just to end up stalled again, five feet from the last place we lurched and stalled.

I hold up my hands, warding off any sound that Porter might make, any instruction, any comment or criticism or useful nugget of wisdom. I don't want to hear it. I look over my shoulder to see my latest batch of little burnouts in the gravel. You can follow my embarrassing path across the lot pretty clearly from bald spot to bald spot.

Afraid that one of these times I am going to lurch us right over the edge and into the quarry, I adjust the rearview mirror and sit up straight. God, how hard can this be?

Start the car. Push in the clutch. I can hear Porter in my head, calmly repeating the instructions, step by step, as I try again. Slowly let out the clutch, and slowly give it some gas.

I feel the pull of the gas before I really have the clutch all the way out. Then the whole car shudders slightly, so I press on the gas hard, harder than I ever did before, so hard I hear loose gravel shooting out behind us as the engine roars and we take off and I am so excited that we are actually moving and that I didn't kill it that I just keep going and going, laying on the gas until I panic and scream, "Porter!"

The edge of the quarry is right there, just over the top of the dash, so I tromp on the brake with both feet, and we come to a violent jerk of a stop, a stop that flings us forward like crash test dummies and leaves me lost in a cloud of blond hair. I can feel the embarrassed flush of my cheeks as I push my hair back, fighting my way out from under the tangle of long golden strands.

Not many people see me this way. Messy. Out of place. Totally out of my element. Failing. I normally participate only in activities I know I can master, activities that my sisters have mastered before me and that I have watched and memorized and been properly groomed for. It's easier that way.

"You do realize that's not my name?" Porter asks quietly as I reach down, avoiding his eyes, and push in the clutch, starting the car again.

Hearing his instructions in my brain and not his voice, really, I slowly let out the clutch as I give it some gas. "What?"

He waits for the inevitable convulsion and then says, "Porter."

I reach down again, push in the clutch again, start the car again, and ask, more loudly this time, "What?"

Over the rumble of the engine, with the clutch in and my right foot revving at the gas, I hear him say clearly, "My name is not Porter."

Surprise pops my foot off the clutch, and I kill the engine, again. Resting my forehead against the steering wheel, I ask, "What are you saying to me?"

He leans forward and snaps the radio off.

"I am saying," he repeats, "my name is not Porter."

But this time he says it real slow and thick, like he is deaf or retarded. Or I am.

I picture the first night we met. See his red jacket. *Porter* is sewn right there, over his heart, in shiny thread that glows gold in my memory. Roger even called him Porter, I remember, and I am pretty sure he responded when Roger called him that. I consider the possibility that maybe he told me his name that night and I forgot it, that it just swirled right out of my brain with all the wine and the making out and rolling around in the soft grass.

I sit still, too confused to get worked up about his tone. The car, the quarry, even my brain get real quiet, and then it hits me. Here I am with this guy again, this guy I have clocked serious intimate time with, and I don't even know his name. God, I could just die. Drive us both off that cliff right over there, plunge us past the pointy rocks and worn-out class of '87 spray paint, graffiti and garbage racing past us, the last things we see on our way to the jagged, silty bottom and our certain deaths. And I don't even know the guy's name. Damn.

When they send someone out from the local paper to cover the tragedy, the headline will read, FUTURE VALEDICTORIAN LEAH JOHNSON AND SOME RANDOM DUDE DIE IN TRAGIC CAR ACCIDENT. There will be the obligatory photo of the mangled muscle car at the bottom of the quarry, with a spiral of smoke drifting up from its sooty black pinstripes. "Yes, she was driving," people will say as they admire the carnage. "Did you even have to ask?"

Giving up my death grip on the wheel, I lean back and shake my head, trying to clear it.

Sighing, I give up completely and ask, "What is your name then?"

"Duffy. Jon Duffy. JD. Your choice."

Duffy?

My eyes grow big, and I suck in a breath as I turn toward him, but before I can even ask, Porter continues in a long, singsongy way. "Yes, I am Jon Duffy, son of Don Duffy, Big Duff, as you probably know him."

Well, of course I know him. Everybody knows him. Big Duff is almost as notorious as Sam, Sam, the UPS man, for nailing every recently separated or divorced woman in town. While Sam trolls town in his brown truck and brown shorts, making "special deliveries," Big Duff works the country club with a five iron and a wicked grin. He is the golf pro at our club and a permanent fixture on the fairways and in the clubhouse.

My dad golfs with him sometimes if he needs someone to fill out a foursome on a late afternoon.

He is a big, burly man with a strong backswing and a boisterous laugh. He may be called Big Duff, but my dad says, "I haven't seen him duff one yet." I'll take his word for it, but secretly I wonder how anyone can swing a club around a stomach that big. Personally, I gave up golf forever when my boobs started getting in the way.

I've seen him in the bar at the club on social nights, talking golf and laughing loudly, his cheeks ruddy and his hairline receding. He usually has one arm wrapped around a tan blonde who comes complete with diamond studs, moisturized crow's-feet, and two teenage sons, while his other hand stirs the limes around in his tall, clear drink.

"Your knees are shaking," Don Duffy's son says, nodding toward my legs.

I look down at them. They look kind of funny, as if they don't belong to my body. Porter, Duffy, Jon Duffy, JD, Big Duff, clutch, gas, brake, clutch. There are too many choices.

Staring straight ahead at the quarry, I say, "I think I've had enough of this."

"You're right."

He shoves his door open, climbs out, and makes his way around the front of the car, his fingertips trailing along the sparkly blue hood as he goes.

He reaches my side. "It is smelling a bit hot," he says.

That's not really what I meant, I think as I sniff at the air, trying to smell the difference between hot engine and hot boy. I didn't mean I've had enough of this driving business, I meant more like I think I've had enough of this who the hell are you business, but here he is already, pulling my door open like a gentleman, and I really don't want to get into it with him, since he's practically a stranger and we are almost straddling a dark and rocky hole perfect for the dumping of dead clutch-challenged teenage girls. Don Duffy's son has decided he should drive, and so it shall be.

I skitter across the gravel to the passenger side. He starts the engine as I slide into my seat, and then I feel it, like a strong yank to my gut—the pull and switch as the clutch lets go and the gas takes over in a perfectly smooth transition under Porter's control, with no pause or gap or reluctance. So, I think as I relax, leaning into the cushioned leather, that's how it's supposed to feel.

We are barely moving, but I need to know before we go any farther or any faster, so I turn to him and ask, "Do you know my name?"

He rolls the car along slowly, the gravel bumping and popping gently underneath the tires. He turns and leans toward me until our foreheads almost touch.

"Yes," he says, smiling, "of course I do." He kisses me on the forehead. "You're Leah."

I don't know how he knows. Did I tell him? I thought I did, and I didn't. I thought he didn't know, but he did.

"Then why does your jacket say Porter?" My finger embroiders some invisible floss into my T-shirt, right above my heart.

"'Cause I am a porter," he says simply as he turns the wheel sharply, pointing us away from the rocks and the danger and toward the hum of the highway. "At the club. It's my job. Park the cars, wash the cars, porter the cars. And you know, occasionally," he smiles over at me as he turns left onto the highway and we finally hit blacktop with a squawk and leave the dusty gravel for good, "drive the cars."

"I guess that explains the cars."

"Yeah, I guess it does," he replies as he shifts into a higher gear and we take off.

The quarry has become a small strip of purple and bronze streaks in the sparkly oval mirror outside my open window when I finally figure it out. Duh, I think as I drop back into my seat, a little bit blown away.

"You looked at my license," I say.

He laughs and takes my hand, rubbing his thumb lightly across my knuckles.

"Smart *and* hot," he says, "Just my type."

I grin, squinting into the sunlight. That's exactly what I was thinking.

Seven

I remember the grass at our old lake house. It was like a green rug, cool and thick, the whole summer through. It was good for running in bare feet, and we had tons of trees. Oaks. Huge ones that made great shade and tree houses and could hold up the three of us tumbled into one hammock with no trouble.

I learned to golf on that sloped front lawn. With his big arms wrapped around mine, my dad helped me line up my shot with my tiny putter, and then we watched the dimpled white ball roll away, over and over, until it was almost too dark to see it in the thick grass.

But this house is too new, the grass started as seed, the trees too young to provide any shade. Some of them are still staked, and we are just hoping they make it through the summer heat. It doesn't help that it hasn't rained in what feels like forever.

I leave the house early each morning. My mother peers over the rim of her latte, spoon resting on the edge of her saucer, because there should *always* be a saucer, gives me a quick visual inspection, and compliments my lip gloss before returning to her bridal magazine. A short lick across her thumb dismisses me as she flicks to the next glossy page, and I am on my way.

The grass crunches and flattens under my feet as I ceremoniously cut a drawn-out sloping angle across our yard, ignoring the buzzing coming from my bag as Dani and Len call yet again, probably after another all-nighter. I avoid our long black driveway for as long as possible and, with it, the imminent early-morning arrival of Roger.

Like clockwork, he downshifts as he makes his military-style turn into our driveway at exactly 8:15 A.M. each day. Exactly.

I overslept once—I think it was after a hard night of fending off Shane—and there I was, still half asleep, propped up in the breakfast nook with my sisters nursing some thick chocolaty milk, when the doorbell rang. I heard my mother's heels click across the foyer and then her voice echoing into the kitchen: "Oh, Roger, you're practically family now . . . no need to ring the bell." Roger shoved himself into the breakfast nook, practically squeezing me out, and leaned over to wrap his arms around Yorke's stomach and give her what I thought was a very sloppy kiss, morning time or not. I almost barfed.

Now I am sure to escape early, and after weeks of practice I can make it all the way across the yard and to the edge of the driveway before I smile big and fake and wave at Roger just as he angles his red car to ninety degrees and snaps down the drive.

Free for the day, I sling my bag and swing my

hips along the path through the park, never sure when and how Porter will show up, but sure that he will. It turns out he was right, he has become a habit.

Each car is different. Every day is new. He just rolls up, *rrvvvvvvvt*, and my life changes. When my butt settles into the warp of someone else's seat, it feels as if Porter and I are starting again, fresh and new.

The smell of a stranger's perfume, the feel of the upholstery, the wrappers and maps and pens and glove box, are a discovery each time. It's a lot like my relationship, if you can call it that, with him.

It's bits and pieces that I stick together in my mind to make a whole. Two hours here and then ten minutes there. Part of a story about his dad that is cut short 'cause the car we are roaming around in is due back, or a long description of the scar that I noticed on his hand and how he got it when he was twelve and wanted to paint his bedroom and tried to open a can of black semigloss with a humongous flat screwdriver that slipped out of the groove and stabbed him in the hand that was trying to hold everything steady.

I know that he and Big Duff don't exactly get along but tolerate each other. That Big Duff walked out on Porter and his mom when Porter was five and then drank himself into a hole. That Big Duff is now clean and sober (surprise to me) and has a toaster oven that he likes to cook personal pizzas in. That Porter has to show him how to do it each and every time. That Porter thinks Big Duff's cigarettes or the toaster oven are going to burn the house down one night.

I have never seen it, the house about to go up in toaster oven flames, but I imagine a leather sofa and matching love seat covered in sloppy vinyl tape Xs that hide the cigarette burns and worn spots. It is very man decorated and has a slight smell, probably from the oversplashing of Big Duff's cologne as he leaves for his dates.

I know that Big Duff does three things religiously—Wednesday night AA meetings, a 6:00 A.M. tee time on Thursdays, and Sunday morning service—and that he is not happy that Porter will not join him in any of the three.

Porter is hard to pin down, so I know how Big Duff feels. He changes cars the way I change outfits or lip gloss. He can appear in a car borrowed from someone at a tennis lesson, or in a Jeep with a fresh buff and wax, even in a gold Mercedes owned by a bronzed trophy wife spending the day in the club spa. I hop in, and Porter slides his arm along the back of the seat, fingers sparking their way across the upholstery before they light onto my tan shoulder and we take off.

I never know where we are going. It could be the park, or the quarry, maybe the lake, or even the curvy road that goes past the bluff. With Porter it seems nothing is out of the way or out of bounds or too far. It's so unpredictable that it's perfect.

One time we spent the morning parked in front of the big screen at the abandoned drive-in theater two towns over. The screen was slashed, but the white Porsche was brand-new. Oddly, the dash, and practically every other surface visible from the driver's seat, was covered in neon-colored Post-it notes, the little teeny, tiny ones that are practically impossible to write on. They were stuck to the odometer, the radio display, and the cup holders. They were everywhere.

I put my feet up on the dash and leaned my head back, laughing as Porter peeled off each note, squinted, and attempted to decipher the elfin handwriting, reading it out loud if he could, before he put the note back in a completely different spot. Later that day I found a bright pink Post-it stuck to the bottom of my sandal. Scratched and dirty, it said simply "Dry cleaning." I folded it up and stashed it away in the front pocket of my backpack. Someone's shirts may be forgotten, but I will remember that day always.

Eight days later we drove for forever in a totally dirty and disgusting Cadillac with green and purple Mardi Gras beads hanging from the rearview mirror and crumbs of unknown origin all over the floor. Running out, doors left open, we dipped our feet into a river three counties away from home, cool and mossy, just to run back up the bank and drive home with dripping ankles in time for Porter to return the car to an old man in plaid golf pants. Porter told me the next day that the guy tipped him fifteen bucks for taking such good care of it.

Sometimes he drives by with only a minute to spare and we get orange juice and powdered sugar doughnuts and make out on the hood of some random car in the parking lot at the Supervalue. He is sticky sweet, and I want to swallow him whole.

I can't imagine how to explain this confusion and anticipation and unexpected delight to anyone, especially to anyone in my family. So for now I don't. I know I am safe because my mother is buried in invitation samples and calligraphy choices and Shane is hidden under a helmet, sweating it up on the fifty-yard line blocks away.

You would think I would be used to it by now, but Porter still leaves me feeling wide awake and trembling. Before, I knew exactly what was going to happen and how and with whom and when. But life with Porter rolls by so fast, a moving feast of kissing and supermarket baked goods and sneaking around.

With Shane it's like someone is leaning on the brakes, hard. We spend our nights stuck, watching movies or minigolfing, where I always win because his hammy hands are too big to maneuver the tiny putter. We eat burgers and fries at the drive-in, the tray resting on his car door, the dripping glass mugs filled with soda, and Shane's hand wet and heavy on my thigh.

I don't fit in Shane's car anymore. And I used to think it was made for me. I know if I angle my head the right way, I can see myself in the visor mirror and the side mirror at the same time. One of my tampons is buried, in case of emergency, in the back of the compact glove box. My hairbrush is tossed onto the backseat. The interior smells of my perfume. I own this guy.

But I find myself pulling at the seat belt now, stretching it out away from me. It is rubbing my neck, chafing me and pressing me too tight into the seat. I struggle, and Shane reaches over, touching my neck, trying to lean in and kiss it, asking, "Here?"

I swat him away, complaining, "It hurts."

He is quicksand. The more I fight, the farther in I fall. I feel caught and confused. Finally I give in and close my eyes.

I see fields and farms rolling by in my mind, the ground soft and dark as little green plants shoot up in the morning sun, a bright smile and bright eyes behind the wheel next to me, the road open and unknown before us.

This road exists in a space that is all mine. I don't have to share it with anyone. It is the most important part of my life but is totally separate from my actual life. It is not one piece of a matching set, it hasn't been done before, I didn't just memorize the steps while watching Freddie's feet tap, tap, tap as the curtain lifted.

When Shane's lips brush against my ear, my eyes pop open and everything skids to a stop. Reality snaps into focus, and I know exactly where this is headed, whether I want it or not—more Friday nights, more fumbling around in the backseat, more sloppy kisses and copped feels and constantly holding hands in the hallway.

I feel like the last car in the Fourth of July parade, the one stuck behind the horses and the high school band, held up by the Hi-Steppers, the local third-grade baton twirlers who, year after year, never actually seem to learn to twirl a baton. I am idling.

Eight

Valerie is officially the color of my mother's morning coffee. Yes, in six weeks she has become a light, cancery brown, the human approximation of a double nonfat mocha with extra foam and two pink packets of sweetener.

I admit, I had my doubts that tanning was even possible for her when she walked into the pool that first day all frail and pasty and white, then walked out later all pink and broiled, but today, as I watch her through the squeaky clean glass of the office window, the cool metallic honeycomb of the pool fence and gray sky as her backdrop, she definitely looks a little less sickly. Who knows? By the end of the summer she could resemble a real person. Maybe.

I grab a pen and quickly scribble my initials onto the wrinkled, water-spotted staff sign-in sheet. It says KEEP IT SAFE OUT THERE! Someone has turned the dot of the exclamation point into the head of a swimmer, drowning in a sea of ballpoint blue waves. A black marker shark swims in to bite his ankles.

I scoop up my rolled towel and whistle and stop to check myself in the mirror hanging next to the peeling door frame. Ignoring the gawking freshman boys watching my every move and Margo with the man voice, I stride across the deck, my suit riding higher with each long, hip-swinging step.

Valerie does an about-face, stalls, and then matches her pace to mine so that we are walking along together. She is wearing white knee socks and those exercise sandal things with a wide-striped halter suit. Ouch. And she wonders why she can't get a date. Actually, I don't know if she wonders that, since we never talk about that kind of stuff. But please, there's her answer. She looks like a broasted chicken with shoes on. *Slip clonk, slip clonk*, her socks and sandals are an evil combo as she tries to keep up with me.

"Shane was looking for you," she says, completely out of breath.

I pretend I don't care and simultaneously wonder if I really even do as I remember in delicious detail the car, the kissing, and the store-bought cinnamon coffee cake that was this morning.

"I told him I didn't know where you were," she says.

Catching her breath, she holds her hand out and takes my towel from me. I pull myself up onto the first rung of the red lifeguard chair. Reaching down, I take my towel back and ask, "Yeah, what did he say?"

"He asked me who I was."

I smile, and she *slip clonks* away.

Troy blows his whistle long and loud, and the

pool splits open with a spectacular cannonball. It's always a cannonball. A ring of sharp waves marks the point of impact as the first kid in finally bobs to the surface, his smile and splash greeted by the whoops and cheers of a clump of skinny-legged third-grade boys. They high-five each other and line up to take turns at cannonballing themselves. One right after the other, knobby knees hugged to bony chests, *pa-wump*, *pa-wump*, *pa-wump*. Their splashes fly high, sprinkling down on my bare thighs as I settle into my shift under a troubled summer sky. The realization that I am now indebted to Valerie sinks in slowly as the cannonball water drools down my legs and pools into a warm puddle at my feet.

The clouds drop lower and lower until they almost brush against the top of my shoulders. I look around the pool. Parents are nervously glancing toward the sky, caught between a few more minutes of peace or dragging a crying kid out of the water. The official rule is sprinkles are safe, but thunder and lightning clear the pool immediately, no exceptions.

Troy is standing on the other side of the pool. He straddles the red 5FT marker, his toes curling over the edge as he watches the sky for lightning. I can practically see his fingers crossing and uncrossing from here. He is hoping, wishing, praying even for a lightning bolt or a clap of thunder. Then he can chill out, roll a fat one, and maybe watch some TV. All around him, even the hopeful are giving up, tying bikini strings, pulling on T-shirts, and packing up sunscreen. It is not going to happen today.

Somewhere behind me, in the quickly dimming light, Valerie is on a frayed Fingerhut beach towel, continuing her assault on anemia and our assigned summer reading list. I crank my head around to look at what she is straining to read, the book just inches from her face. *April Morning*. Right. Something about a boy and a war, maybe even some drums. I haven't read it and have no plans to. Why would I? I have two older sisters. We live in a small town with a tiny school system. The same teachers have been teaching the same classes and assigning the same texts since the dawn of time. My copy, complete with Yorke's faded yellow highlights and Freddie's meticulous notes neatly written in the margins, is just waiting for me at home. I'm all set.

But Valerie is plowing through it, page by flipping page. This book and the entire summer reading list, too. She has a ritual. Each day she unpacks the books and stacks them up. The finished ones are placed to her left with a little pat. Then those about to be tackled are arranged, most likely in alphabetical order, to her right.

There's no way I would schlep all those books around all summer, but Valerie does. I want to admire her spirit. I do, but I am finding it hard to look past her spine as it bumps and curves over that mountain of reading material.

Her bid for valedictorian, her hard work, it's all there, printed and bound and stacked up for me to see. I can almost make out one of the titles from up here: *Guilt. Now Available in Paperback!* I turn, twisting to face the water again.

At the first crack of thunder, I jump up, knees locking, and blow my whistle, joining the four other lifeguards shrilly clearing the pool. Moms panic and grab kids. It's a little like *Jaws*, but without the screaming or the mechanical shark.

The place clears in about five minutes. Striped towels? Gone. Bicycle racks? Empty. Pool? Flat and still. It is amazing how fast people will move when they are about to be rained on, especially when most of them are already wet. Out of the corner of my eye I see Troy stretch his arms up toward the sky and clap his hands over his head. God, he's such a burnout.

Of course Valerie is the last to leave. I am already outside the fence, sitting on the hill, shoes off, chin resting on my knees as I wait for my ride, while she dawdles, kneeling on the concrete pool deck, frantically cramming her many, many, many books into her striped canvas tote.

She is always the last one in the school hallways at the final bell, too, pissing off the janitor and the teacher who just wants to stop answering her questions and go home. Right now she is pissing off Troy.

I lower my forehead to rest on my crossed arms and curl up tight against the wind. Eons pass, and then I finally hear Troy's keys jangling, the lock twisting, and the clank of the gate. The pool is closed.

"Alas! Here we see her, our fair Leah. Left behind, yet waiting patiently, ever faithful, ever hopeful, for her knight in shining armor."

I lift my chin to find Valerie standing before me, orating like the Greek chorus. Thing is, I don't really need the recap. I can feel the cold, scratchy grass beneath my ass right now, so I get it. I am living it.

Maybe Valerie's been speed-reading too much Shakespeare. Ignoring her as she walks to her car, I search every set of headlights in the distance for the one that is coming for me.

With an overly dramatic flourish of her free hand and a less than graceful curtsy that is hampered by her heavy book bag, Valerie stops next to her German rust bucket and calls, "Do you need a ride?"

Nice, but yeah, right. I can just see us together, Valerie behind the wheel and me riding shotgun.

"Umm . . . thanks, but I'm sure Shane will show."

"Shane?" she says with a humph as she props her door open with her skinny hip and throws her book bag across the seat with both hands, granny style. A spring squeaks loudly when it lands. After climbing into the driver's seat, she pulls the creaky door shut and leans out the open window with a sly smile.

"You sure that's who you're hoping for?" she asks before she backs up in a series of rolling jerks, momentarily blinding me when she flips on her headlights during jerk number two. She waves and drives off into the gathering storm. My feet are cold, my butt is sore, and the sky is as dark as night, practically. Turning away, I don't wave back at her. I just see spots.

The air today is even more oppressive than my mood. I can feel it all around me as I give up and start to walk home through the park. The tall green grass at the edge of the road dips, lies flat, and then snaps back to attention. The trees swaying in the strengthening wind seem too fragile; they bend toward me at an impossible angle, and the headlights that suddenly pop over the crest of the hill are too bright and piercing against the greenish gray horizon. I step up my pace. A short, muffled yell in the distance stops my heart and slows my feet for a second. I'm sure it was just someone calling for a dog or a kid or, you know, warning me that the end is near. I lean into the wind, heart flying, cursing my parents, my sisters, Shane, even Porter a little bit, for leaving me out here. Adrift.

I am winding my way through the flower garden, lush and tall and muggy, when the wind suddenly shifts, lifting my hair and swirling it into my face. I stumble, losing my step and my place. I trip over a slab of uneven sidewalk and land with a short skid on the concrete path, backpack jilted to one side, the skin rubbed raw on the heel of my right hand, my hair still in my face. I reach up, instinctively, looking for a hand to hold, someone to pull me up, to pull me along and show me which way to go. There's no hand, only the sharp sting of my raw skin in the cooling air.

Flowers tower over me, bobbing and weaving. Leaning back, I watch them, delicate and bright against the dark sky, and discover that I am sheltered under a canopy of blue and yellow and pink blooms. They dance above me, filling this calm little enclave I have landed in with the smell of summertime. I breathe in, long, steady breaths that fill my lungs with the perfume of picnics and parks and pools, of bike rides and T-ball practice, bouquets of dandelions, of sunshine and my sisters. Pressing down on my scraped hand to kill the last of the sting there, I collect myself, and my stuff, and set out again for home. I know the way by heart.

At the top of our driveway, lined up in a neat row, safe and dry, I see them—RGR DGR, LHS BUG, SHN ROX. How annoying. No wonder people hate us. I trail my finger along the waxed and shiny and professionally detailed trunks, taunting the threatening skies to open up and do their worst.

A few feet away, our kitchen window is a big glowing square. I stop, watching the scene play out on the other side of the thick glass. Like an actress on a TV with the sound turned off, Yorke talks with her mouth big and wide, her hands animated. Whatever she has to say is always the most important thing at that moment.

My mother and Freddie are at the table in the nook, lost in a landslide of RSVP cards and sample place settings. Freddie's got a clipboard and a pen. She lifts a thick, engraved card from the pile, makes a check mark, and then puts the card into another pile. Repeat. My mother seems to be doing nothing more than arranging the large, sliding pile into smaller, neater piles, probably so the cards won't knock over the etched champagne flutes. And Yorke just keeps talking.

There's an empty chair next to Freddie, waiting for me. I'm sure I could help Freddie with that list. I could check off the names while she reads them off the cards, or the other way around. Either way we always make a good team.

The wind swirls to a stop, and the air is suddenly still, so still and silent that the hair on my arms stands up. I pause, looking through the window at my life one year from now, two years from now, twenty-five years from now. It looks perfect from out here.

Yorke is planning the perfect wedding, and then she'll move away with Roger. Freddie will parse some more French verbs, perfectly, be maid of honor, and go off to France for a year. But what about me? I think, What am I doing? Not Shane, that's for sure.

He's there, too, sunken into our creamy leather sofa, feet up on the ottoman, the two in his two-a-day obviously canceled because of the weather. Shane is part of the perfect supporting cast: dark-haired men, fit and tan, with white teeth and white shirts, watching a game that I can't hear, the TV flickering silently.

I take a few steps back, away from the house, feeling obvious and out of place in the dead, dark quiet. All I have to do is open the door and step inside, but I'm confused. Why am I on the outside looking in?

I want to go in and take my place, safe and

secure, at the end of the line, right next to Freddie, blue, then yellow, then pink. But I want to walk away, too. Right past this house, out of the yard, down the street, past the high school and homecoming queen and sweaty nights in Shane's backseat. Past the valedictorian speech complete with Valerie's condemning glare and my parents' pride. Past my trip abroad, France most likely, and my college dorm room with a bright, cheery bedspread, my future sorority sisters, and the unknown boy, with dark hair and a bright future growing up somewhere right now, who will take me off my parents' hands in, according to schedule, exactly three years.

Freddie reaches up and slides her long blond hair back behind one ear with a slight flick, a familiar motion. Unconsciously I reach up to do the same and stop myself, suddenly remembering a day like this, with the same eerie stillness, the air just as thick, when we were little and taking riding lessons.

Our lesson was cut short when the weather shifted, so we brushed the brown, shiny horses and locked them safely in their stalls. As the thunderclouds boiled outside the barn, the normally sedate horses grew skittish and uneasy. Their eyes got big. Their tails switched. Circling their stalls faster and faster, they bucked against the boards, desperate for a way to get out. I was scared. Yorke was indignant. Freddie was smart and had stayed home that day.

Feeling as restless and unsettled as those penned ponies, I watch the lightning scratching away at the edges of the dark sky and think, Batten down the hatches, some shit is about to go down. The first raindrops start to fall fast and thick, and before they can even hit the ground and be swallowed up by the parched dirt, before they can break the dull silence and splat, fat and wet on the driveway, making heads turn and look my way in anger or concern or surprise, I bolt.

I make my way back to the park, picking my way through puddles and the patches of darkness. It's raining so hard that the ground can't keep up. Rivers of sticks and leaves and grass turn and tumble on top of the dust before waterfalling over the curbs and rushing out into the street. Rain-filled gutters blubber and boil over like a summer soup. My feet fight against the current that snakes toward a storm sewer somewhere behind me as I walk along the edge of the road.

Please, please, please, I breathe, please, please, please. This patter fills my head between the rolls of thunder drumming like timpani. Squinting against the bolts of lightning, I flinch every single time a drop of rain smacks onto my face, sharp and cold. Step by step, I squint, I flinch, I pray. It's worse than facing down a nasty crowd throwing nickels and quarters and assorted loose change from the stands during halftime. Ouch. At least out on the field you can hide behind a set of poms or an unlucky freshman. Out here I'm alone. It's just me, jumpy, cold, and wet. And crying. God, I hope no one sees me.

The sound of tires on wet blacktop stops my forward march. Bright lights, white paint. My heart drops, sure that it's Shane. I lower my head to wipe away my tears and realize that it's pointless.

It's raining, right? Looking up between my dark, dripping lashes, I see him. My cheeks flush, and my heart does double time. Tossing my head back, I laugh and swallow my tears. My soggy little rain-soaked prayers have been answered. By a hot guy in a huge white truck. Bonus.

I cross the river of rainwater between us and tiptoe toward the truck. I swear that steam is rising off me when I step up to the driver's window and cling onto the wet rubber ledge. Up on my toes, I lean in, lips pursed. Then I change my mind, switch gears, and decide to get it right this time.

"Duffy," I say, and breathe out with a shy smile, almost embarrassed to be using his name for the first time.

He leans his head back against the seat and laughs as the rain drums against the solid metal of the truck.

"You decided," he says. A "finally" is kind of implied.

"Yes."

I lift my hand and swipe my wet hair across

my forehead to stop the drips from rolling into my eyes as I nervously ramble on, "And it was difficult." Counting off on my wrinkled fingers, I run through the choices for him, "Jon—too plain, not you. And Jon Duffy, well, that's a bit formal for us . . . isn't it?" I look into his eyes to see if it really is before I continue. Yep, it is. "And Porter, well, you know how that one goes." He nods because he does know. "And JD." I sigh and shake my head before quickly saying, "Well, JD sounds like something from *The Dukes of Hazzard*." His quizzical look keeps me explaining, and I draw an imaginary line with my finger through the rain right above my waist and clarify, "You know, from below the Mason-Dixon line."

He grins. "Been there," he says, looking down.

"Yeah, well," I grab his chin and drag his eyes back to mine, "the North wins."

He holds his hands up and concedes with a smile, then leans past the green glow of the dash lights and almost disappears for a second when he stretches to grab the latch on the passenger door, letting me in.

Slippery, wet, and shivery, I scramble toward the other side of the truck and stumble and slip on the high step up. I look across the cab, and those intense green eyes melt me like flux as they take in every movement I make, my clinging T-shirt, my plastered shorts, every drenched bit of me. His hand reaches out to steady me, and I slide into the seat, a puddle of rainwater and anticipation.

Duffy busies himself, playing with the heater, turning the dial quickly to set it on blast furnace, adjusting all the slats and vents to point directly at me, while I take a look around at the gray plaid interior of the truck. A collection of shorty pencils lines the foggy crack between the dash and the windshield and a fuzzy gray golf club cover hides the stick shift.

I have a feeling that this might be Big Duff's truck. It smells exactly like the cologne aisle in the drugstore downtown, woodsy and a little bit cheap, but potent, just like Big Duff. I pull a half-swamped piece of paper from under my left butt cheek and smooth it out with my damp hands. It's last week's church bulletin. That and the overflowing ashtray make me think, Yep, it's got to be.

"Is-Is this—" I stammer because I can't bring myself to say it, to use the words Big Duff, 'cause that would make the smoldering guy dropping into reverse next to me Little Duff, which has so many negative implications and is, honestly, too close for comfort to Little Johnson for me. So instead, with a little residual teeth chattering, I ask, "Is this your dad's truck?"

He flips up the lid on the boxy fake leather console between us, reaches in, and pulls out a handful of thick, supersoft cream-colored paper towels.

"Yep," he says. He hands them over and shifts into second with the wipers set on high.

I wipe the rain and the last traces of my mascara from my cheeks, leaving dark black smears across the bold gold script running along the edge of the towel, COMPLIMENTS OF HILLPOINT COUNTRY CLUB.

The tobacco-scented heat blasts away as we drive through the empty park, past the high school and the country club, down endless country roads, soaked and stormy, a thick trench of rain rolling out in our wake.

I get the feeling we are going farther tonight than we ever have before. The wipers keep time with the classic rock on Big Duff's car stereo, the fan heating so high and loud that we can barely talk above it. I rest my head against my window. Rain streaks by on the glass, creeping past my eyes and disappearing behind me, back toward town, where I'm sure someone, maybe everyone, must be looking for me, wondering where I am, worried, knowing that the pool is closed and I should be home by now.

They can always call if they are so desperate. I'm sure my phone is somewhere in the bottom of my soggy backpack. I don't bother to check it. Instead I let the rain lull me. It dodges and slides along the glass as we drive on, taking with it any guilty thoughts of Shane or my family that linger in my head and I think I could go on like this forever, wrapped in a safe little womb of moving warmness, music, and Porter. Um, I mean, Duffy.

The rain finally stops, dwindling to a heavy mist that clings to everything and leaves the windows so foggy that I have to crack mine open just to see out when Duffy starts to slow down, driving the truck into a clearing somewhere on top of a low, wide hill. He pulls right up to the base of some wooden stairs. I lean out and look up. The stairs wind around and around up the sides of a tall, square wooden tower with four platforms, the top one so high it's lost in the dark slate sky.

"I want to show you something," Duffy says as he kills the engine and the lights.

He reaches for my hand, and I slide out of the high truck. He pulls me to him as we dash through the long, wet grass and start to climb the thick plank steps. It crosses my mind that climbing a tall tower in the middle of nowhere just after a thunderstorm is probably not totally safe, but I don't feel scared with his hand holding mine, pulling me along. Up and up, his work boots clomp on the stairs, setting the pace in the semidarkness. A step behind, I depend on their sound and the trailing swish of the red nylon jacket tied loosely around his waist to lead the way.

I stop short when we get to the very top of the steps and the final platform. I drop his hand. My world is spread out before me, a broad skyline of tall trees and small towns separated by dark, open spaces. How is it possible that I have never seen this before? Never been here? I turn, speechless, wondering at the view from each side of the tower. We can't be more than a couple of counties over.

"My mom used to bring me up here," Duffy says as I step up next to him, "when I was little." He turns toward me with a small smile, his green eyes reflecting back a bright bolt of lightning piercing the sky somewhere behind me.

I watch him closely. This is the first time he has ever mentioned his mother. He's letting me in, a little bit at a time, first with the truck and now this, and I am not sure what to say. I walk to the edge of the platform and hold tight to the wooden railing. Under my fingers I can feel the scrapes and scratches of initials and other gouged graffiti in the splintery wood.

I lift my face and watch the sky, twinkling with the lights from houses in some places, cloudy and streaking with distant lightning in others. Duffy moves in behind me quietly, close and warm. His hands straddle mine on the railing, his body blocking the wind and rooting me to the spot, breathless. We look out over the patchwork of freshly washed small towns below us. My blood runs hot and quick through my veins, pulsing at my temples and the base of my neck. I lean into him, feel his arms wrap around me tight as he slowly turns me to face him, the air tense and thick between us. He lifts my chin with his hand and then . . . rain, heavy and sudden. Dumping down on us.

Duffy grabs my hand and pulls me across the platform and down one flight of stairs so quickly I don't even feel the steps under my feet. Panting and laughing, I rush in and kiss him, warm and wet, and we fumble and slip down to the floor, dry as kindling under the shelter of the top platform. There's no music or soft car seat underneath me, just raw lumber, the sound of rain, and hard, hungry kisses.

I am shivering all over. Duffy stops, leaning up on one elbow, his fingers trailing lightly across my shaky stomach and asks, "Cold?"

Yeah, that's it, I think as I nod my head, knowing that it's not, 'cause all those nights with Shane I have never done anything like this. Not even close, really. He reaches behind him and grabs his slippery red jacket. I sit up, and he puts it under me, Porter side down, fleecy white fabric rubbing softly against my bare back as I relax into it. He stretches out, pressing up against the length of my body. It feels as if our friction could spark in the air, and I know what I want to do. The storm presses in around us, silencing our sounds and separating us from the world below as the edges of the sky flare again and again with lightning that reaches down like long fingers, searing into the dark, wet ground.

Nine

The morning air slipping through my curtains feels cool against my fingers as I reach up to touch a fluttering hem. The rain outside sounds soft and gentle, a soft beat against the patio and the rooftop. The storm has passed, and it smells like worms.

I roll over, untangling my legs from the duvet and rub my fingers lightly over my scraped shoulder blade, wincing a little. I close my eyes, feeling safe and snug in the tight cotton weave of my tank top, daring myself to drift back to sleep, to dream of Duffy and ignore my pissed-off parents and the inevitable punishment I know is waiting for me below.

"Leah, get your ass down here!" Yorke blares from downstairs. The smell of coffee curls under my door. I am awake.

It wasn't that late when I got home. Seriously. It just felt late since it had been dark since breakfast, practically.

"Where is she?" I asked as I dropped my soggy backpack onto the floor with a squish.

Yorke and Freddie were seated around the island in our kitchen, elbows on the granite, stools pulled in close, filling little lace sachet bags with confetti. They scooped and filled, handing over the bulging little bags to Roger for tying and stacking. Roger was tying little white bows faster than any man should be able to tie little white bows.

Yorke pointed up at the ceiling, and my eyes trailed along the smooth white plaster, imagining the *shink, shink, shink* of my mother and her bracelets as they made their way down the hall toward her bedroom.

"Shane's out looking for you," Yorke said, scooping into the confetti with her eyes trained on me.

"Why?" I asked, acting nonchalant. "I'm here."

"'Cause your shift is over and you're supposed to need a ride home," she said, swirling the sparkles in the bowl with her breath.

"Umm," I glanced over at the window. "It's been raining for hours."

"Really?" Yorke asked, sounding surprised.

"Storming, actually," I said, and she craned her neck to look out the window at the gray sky and dripping window screens.

Freddie did not look. She knew it was raining, just like she knows everything. Roger seemed too busy getting his fingers around a slippery ribbon to realize we were even talking, let alone notice the weather.

"Oh, right," Yorke said, "look at that."

She turned back to me with a hungry glint in her eyes and asked, "Where have you been, then?"

Crap. Caught by my own competitiveness. I shouldn't have pointed out the weather. I should have sauntered by and escaped to the solitude of my room and the softness of my bed. They might never have even noticed I'd gone missing.

"Yes, Miss Leah," my mother said as she walked into the kitchen, wearing a bright yellow embroidered tunic and crisp white capri pants. I swear the woman does not wrinkle. A cloud of Chanel No. 5 followed her. "Where have you been?"

I stood, mouth open, not at all prepared for the onslaught. A good excuse or escape plan had never crossed my mind.

I've been in trouble before for stuff like being late to dinner or not cleaning up before Silvia, the cleaning lady, was due, but I have never felt the wrath. Not really, not like Yorke has. I looked over at Yorke with pleading eyes—help me. Yorke just smiled and kept filling those little bags. Apparently I was on my own.

"I know you know how to use a telephone," my mother said as she reached into her purse and pulled out a shiny silver lipstick. "Yet you didn't call."

Truth is, I don't really pay much attention to my cell phone anymore. The one person I want to call doesn't believe in cell phones. Only drive-bys. But I can't tell her that.

"Now poor Shane is out looking for you." She continued, rubbing her newly coraled lips together and dropping the lipstick back into her bag. She glanced at the window. "And it appears to be raining."

God, does anyone in my family ever look past themselves and maybe out a window or something once in a while? I might get over the fact that they didn't miss me too much, but how could they miss what might just have been the best storm ever?

"Well?" my mother asked, her foot tapping on the tile, her arms crossed. "I'm waiting."

"Beg for mercy," Yorke said.

"Save yourself," Freddie teased as she handed another sparkling bag to Roger, her fingers glittery.

"Learn to drive," Roger said baldly as he tied and tossed another filled bag onto the tottering pile.

Yorke swatted at him, halfheartedly. He ducked out of the way and chuckled, annoyingly deep and low.

"I can drive!" I yelled.

"Leah!" my dad bellowed as he walked into the room, freshly shaven, patting at his pockets absentmindedly, looking for his always disappearing set of car keys.

"Pipe down, you three," my mother said. She dropped her set of keys into my dad's open hand and swung her bag up onto her shoulder before she turned toward me with a tight face, expecting an answer.

I sucked in my breath and let it all out with a whoosh.

"Yeah, well," I stalled as I brushed past her, "I was waiting, too, and nobody showed."

I pulled a stool up next to Yorke and reached for an empty sachet. "I had to beg a ride from Valerie."

"Who's Valerie?" Yorke asked. She drew the name out as she said it, stretching the vowels and wrinkling her nose, as if the letters somehow smelled bad.

"A friend." I lied.

"From the pool," I added, and Freddie tilted her head at me, her scoop paused above the bowl. Of course she remembered Valerie. Freddie secretly has her eye on anyone with a superhigh IQ.

I cringed, realizing I shouldn't have added that last bit about the pool. My story would have gone down better without it.

"And the hours between then and now?" my mother asked.

"Studying." I shook the little bag open. "Summer reading list."

I saw Freddie's eyes roll, and even Yorke looked suspicious.

"Seriously," I said as earnestly as I could, and my mother sighed, looking resigned.

"We're going to be late," she said when my dad honked the horn from the driveway.

I tensed as she leaned toward me. She held my chin and looked me dead in the eyes.

"I'll deal with you in the morning," she said. Then she gave me a short, dry kiss on the cheek and walked out the door.

❤ ❤ ❤

"Very sneaky, sis," Yorke said as she stepped into the bathroom that Freddie and I share later that night. Freddie and I were at the double sinks, hair twisted up into ponytails, faces freshly scrubbed.

"Don't you have your own bathroom?" I asked, glancing up at her reflection while twisting the cap off the toothpaste.

"Yes," she sighed, "but it's not nearly as exciting or drama filled as this one."

"No drama, no excitement," I said, gripping the tube of toothpaste directly in the middle because I know it drives Freddie nuts. She likes to work her way up from the end, inch by inch.

Yorke smirked at me in the mirror. "Nice try. Now spill."

I shrugged. "I was out."

"With who?"

"Someone."

"A boy?"

I rolled my eyes, squeezing a straight line of bright blue toothpaste down the length of my bristles.

Freddie looked up from her scrubbing bubbles.

Start brushing, stop talking, I thought, pausing with my mouth open. My toothbrush was just inches from my teeth, but I was reluctant to brush the taste of him off my tongue.

I could feel Yorke watching me intently in the mirror.

"That's it, isn't it?" she concluded.

"A boy." Freddie confirmed softly.

Eyes down, focusing on the swirl of water in the sink, I nodded.

They are a good team. They can get anything out of me, and they know it.

"A little somethin' on the side?" Yorke laughed, the sleeves of her shorty robe shaking as she put her hands on her hips, and I immediately wanted to take back my admission. Regret burned through my brain.

I stood up straight. Talking about him for just a few quick seconds with my sisters was already dulling the experience, taking the shine off and leaving a layer of corrosion behind.

"I didn't think you had it in you," Yorke said to

me, as if it were something to be proud of.

When Yorke was in high school, when she was dating Dwight, her one and only, we came home one Friday night from dinner at a dark and smoky steakhouse. I don't know why Yorke didn't have to suffer through the two hours of drinks, appetizers, dinner, dessert, *and* coffee, but she didn't. Probably lied her way out of it, knowing her.

My dad pulled into our driveway and almost rear-ended a station wagon with fake wooden sides that was parked with the lights off. We rolled up from behind, and Yorke's blue eyes flashed wide from the passenger seat. My mother was out of the car in a second. She pulled the paneled door open and yanked Yorke out by the arm. Yorke stumbled and pulled away. My mother held on tight and led her up the driveway as Freddie and I watched in horror from the backseat, the entire scene illuminated by our headlights.

We saw Yorke turn back and wave at the boy from the next town with tears in her eyes, as if she were devastated. She and Dwight went to prom the next night. I remember Yorke's eyes were still a little puffy. You can see it in the pictures.

"Where were you?" Yorke asked now, demanding, as always. "What did you do? What were you thinking?"

"Who is he?" Freddie asked simply, eyes locked on mine in the mirror.

Yorke will ask more questions, but Freddie will get directly to the point.

I looked up, surprised. I guess they didn't even notice him at the club. How is that possible? It felt as if there were sparks shooting between us. In my mind he practically glows.

"Nobody."

Yorke rolled her eyes.

"You don't know him."

"Hmm . . ." Yorke mulled it over, tossing a hand towel at me. "Then he hardly sounds worth the hell you are going to pay."

Freddie dried her hands, put her toothbrush into the ceramic holder, and folded her towel into thirds before hanging it neatly on the rack by the door.

"He is," I said, and Freddie paused, looking back

at me for a second with a solemn face, before she turned, passed Yorke, and walked out of the room.

"Just wait," Yorke said, shaking her head in a way that sent a shiver down my spine.

She pushed herself up and away from the door frame and clicked off the light.

"He is," I repeated to myself in the darkness, wanting to believe.

"I know, I know, I'm totally late," I say as I drag myself across the kitchen.

"And totally grounded, I bet," Yorke says from the breakfast nook.

"Totally," Freddie adds, sounding very Valley girl. She's propped against the counter, licking honey from the corner of her mouth as I pass by her.

Breakfast is done. I missed it. All that is left is the smell of my dad's fried eggs and some toast crumbs on the counter.

I slide sideways into the nook, shoving up against Yorke. She is nursing her daily cup of caramel-colored coffee, decaf only. The torn pink wrappers from two packets of fake sugar are wrinkled up into a pile in front of her.

"Jesus, Leah," she says when I bump up against her.

I grab the heavy sterling silver dagger of a letter opener off the table and slice an envelope open in one swift movement, *shwish*.

The running total is 233. And each morning the mail brings a fresh batch of RSVPs.

Freddie pours herself a mug of hot coffee, slides into place next to me, and takes up the dark pink pen reserved just for this occasion, crossing another doctor, high school friend, former college roommate, or old lake house neighbor off the long list with a scratch.

"Valerie Dickens?" I say, in shock, reading the reply card in my hand. God, this is a small town. She wants the fish.

"She's Roger's second cousin," Freddie says. "Thought you would know that, being friends and all."

I hear a *shink* as my mother's hand hits the

banister at the top of the stairs, and my pulse quickens. Yorke tilts her head, listening intently, as if it's totally obvious from the sound of my mother's footsteps how much trouble I am in.

"She's pissed," she whispers, and I guess she should know, she's been in more trouble than anyone else in this family. She also has terrible coffee breath.

I lift one of last night's little tied sachets from the pile and give it a limp toss into a box at the end of the table. Two points. Freddie grabs one and lands a three-pointer, unable to resist the urge to outdo me at every turn, even in my time of need.

My mother walks in, still in her satiny slippers but, somehow, with perfect straight-from-the-salon hair. I sometimes think she must sleep sitting up, propped up by gigantic pillows and tiny little dogs, like the Tudors. She stops at the end of the table, blocking any and all exits, and holds up her hands defensively.

"I don't want to hear it," she says sharply.

My mouth, just forming around an appeal, snaps shut so quickly my teeth make a hard little clacking noise.

I notice that Yorke is suddenly focused, all her attention devoted to folding and unfolding one of the pink sweetener wrappers. She smooths it against the table with her thumb before she crinkles it up and starts all over again, leaving a tiny drift of fake sugar in her wake. Freddie's head is down, and she is dropping sachets into the box with such concentration that she could be cramming for a final.

"You will go straight to your job and then come straight home," my mother says as she extends one perfectly manicured finger in my direction.

"No dawdling," she continues, "no field trips, no unexplained absences."

It isn't ugly. Her voice never rises, it never gets loud, but it certainly is painful. Each commandment, every word, lands heavy, a thudding sledgehammer, knocking me lower and lower in the breakfast nook. I am stunned into submission.

I slip below the surface of the table and watch Yorke's foot swing frantically back and forth, her sandal dangling, hanging on for dear life to a polished toe. Freddie's wrapping her legs up like a pretzel, twisting them onto the bench, feet tucked in, toes twitching.

"Wherever you need to go," my mother pauses and looks at each one of us in turn, "Yorke, or Freddie, or Shane can drive you."

Yorke groans loudly but is too afraid of the swirling tempest to bitch in earnest. Freddie groans, too, obviously a card-carrying member of the abused older sisters' union.

My mother shuts them up with a look and adds, "Or I will drive you myself, if necessary."

She lifts her eyebrows at me and, with a tilt of her head in my direction, stalks off, clearly indicating that there will be no arguing or negotiation of terms.

"You *will* be here when I expect you to be, Leah," she says over her shoulder as she heads across the kitchen.

"You will have your priorities straight." She

continues, attacking the already shining faucet with a starched white dish towel. "Shane out on a wild-goose chase in a rainstorm looking for you. What nonsense."

I'd groan, but I can't seem to summon the angst or the energy.

"You act like we don't have a wedding in a few weeks," she says, looking back over at me, past the gleaming granite countertops, over the tops of the polished canisters. Somewhere between the sugar, the salt, the tea, and my perfect sisters, she finds me. I am so low I am practically parallel to the floor.

She waves the dish towel at me, "And for heaven's sake, sit up straight! Bridesmaids don't slump!"

At least not the ones in this family, I think as I hook my elbows heavily onto the edge of the table and pull myself up slowly, until I am proper and straight, surrounded by sisters, like bookends on both sides.

Ten

The temperature took a hit yesterday after the storm and shows no sign of rising up off the mat. Still, Shane has the top down, like always.

"Isn't that your friend?" he asks, grabbing the back of my seat and straining to look past my head as he makes an illegal U-turn and pulls into a handicapped spot.

Afternoons are usually splashing room only this late in the summer, but not today, it appears. Troy is up on a chair near the office, one knee bouncing up and down to stay alert.

"Who?" I ask, my eyes scanning the sparse crowd quickly, looking for the same person I am always looking for.

"Penny . . . ?" he says, totally guessing.

Like I would have a friend named after a coin.

I raise a brow at him.

"It was something with a Y," he says.

"Valerie?" I ask.

"Yeah."

That's my Shane, football hero, heartbreaker, and champion speller.

"She's not my friend," I say. I grab my bag and reach for the door.

Shane grabs me, pulling me in for a kiss that is all hands and hair product. Begrudgingly, I lean over, stiff and awkward, and his fingertips graze my shoulder blade, sliding across the sore spot from last night. I squeeze my eyes tight, and random scenes, lit by bright pops and bursts of lightning, appear in my head. A deep shiver starts in my stomach. It runs down my spine and races through me, scorching my skin, making the kiss even more uncomfortable, but at least it keeps it short. With a dry mouth and a shaky pulse, I pull away.

"I thought you were studying with her yesterday," Shane asks, lifting his chin toward Valerie, his lips pouty, "during the storm."

"Oh, right."

She is leaning against the chain-link fence. An open book is propped against her stomach, pulling her dress tight against her thin chest.

"She's still not my friend," I say. Not even close. She's more like an archnemesis and a social secretary rolled into one.

Valerie shifts, the breeze catching the yellow scarf tied in her hair. She looks up, finds me looking at her, and waves as if we were long-lost friends. Like a fool, Shane waves back, his insincere smile big and white even on this cool gray day.

Valerie's arm droops, and in that same instant so does my heart. Over the rise, leaning up against the hood of a maroon German station wagon that most likely belongs to some unwitting spoiled soccer mom, long legs splayed out in front of him, arms crossed over a worn T-shirt, a sea of grass between us, is Duffy.

I spill out of Shane's car and hardly even notice him pulling away with a wave. He squeals off, spraying pea gravel at my heels.

I climb the slope with my head down, moving as fast as I can. I pass the pool, I pass Valerie, panic pulsing at my temples. I wish that boy with the jumpsuit and the juvie record would swing by right now with his big mower and clear a path for me. I look around for him, hopeful, and instead see Duffy. He is backing up, preparing to drive away.

I slide down the hill at breakneck speed, scrambling, suffocating, and cracking. I trip my way up to the car, trying to read Duffy's expression and catch my breath at the same time.

"Who's the guy, Leah?"

I stop. Silent.

"Girlie white convertible?" he prompts, and I swallow the lump in my throat, watching his knuckles gripping tight and white on the steering wheel.

"Shane," I say slowly and lowly.

"Right," he says, and he stares out his open window, not looking at me but looking at the ground or the grass or something.

"And who's Shane?" he asks.

"My boyfriend."

"You have a boyfriend."

It wasn't a question. He didn't ask. He just kind of said it.

I nod.

"I see. And Shane *rocks*."

I picture the soft tan leather inside Shane's car, the obnoxious shining silver rims, and the polished chrome box frame around the vanity plates, SHN ROX. I shrug.

"Does he?" he asks, his voice rough and angry now. "Does he really rock?"

"Not really."

He just looks at me. "Then what are you doing?"

"I don't know," I say. And really, I don't. It's like I just found out the world is round. I am still feeling around for the edges.

"So, you're cheating."

I am not cheating, I think. Can I cheat on someone that I am not, technically, even going out with? I watch an old couple in red bicycle helmets chugging up the park hill like candy apples.

"I am not cheating," I say clearly. I am certain of that. But with a long, raggedy breath I search for what I actually am doing.

"I am undecided," I conclude.

"What's the difference?" he asks sarcastically, looking up so that I can finally see his eyes.

"Intent."

Duffy rakes his hair back, shaking his head, taking this in.

Finally he clears his throat and asks, "How come you never talk about him?"

Why would I talk about Shane? What is there to say? He is a block of cheese. Thick and square, carved from the same slab as Roger and Evan.

"Well, we never really talk about anything, do we?" I ask. "We just . . . go," I say, swallowing hard, trying to explain, and my heart starts to pull apart, tearing at the edges, and my hands fly toward the horizon, demonstrating our exodus, shaky and nervous with the realization that this might be it.

I can't breathe properly. And I feel like I can't see. The sun breaks through the branches above me, shining between the leaves in pieces and parts, a golden puzzle on my arm, but it doesn't warm my skin. I am numb.

I drop my hands. Tears roll down my face, and I quietly ask, "Can't we just go?"

He nods, yielding.

A trail of cinnamon and sugar shimmers on the dash. Duffy drives, staring straight ahead, taking his time, chewing slowly, a six-pack of doughnuts between us on the front seat, until the words finally rush out of him in a flood.

Turns out that he is going to be a senior this coming fall. At my school. Even though he is already eighteen. He missed a year.

"An entire *year*?" I ask, and he nods, turning

left onto an unmarked road and grabbing another doughnut from the open box.

Not because of stupidity or slacking off, but because his mom was sick. He spent all of last year with her, and that is why he is behind. And why he lives with Big Duff, his dad, now, because his mom died.

"*Cancer*," he says, tight and short, stopping my breath and answering all my questions with a word.

He puts the station wagon into park. Sitting up straight and still, he stares out the windshield, the muscle in his jaw working silently under his skin.

He turns to me with the smile I know so well and says, "So, what's your story?"

But I am unwilling to dive in. Nothing I have can compare with what he's just said. Besides, everyone already knows my story by heart.

The blond ambition, the list of ample goods, the expected test scores, the perfect boys and form-fitting outfits, the high kicks and the constant smile (don't forget about that one), they've all been achieved, first by Yorke and then by Freddie. I am an also-ran.

Duffy reaches over, and his fingers tingle onto my kneecap, wiggling my leg back and forth, prompting me.

I shake my head and say, "It's already been told."

He raises his eyebrows, disbelieving.

"At least twice," I say. "Just look at my sisters."

"That can't be true," he says to me. Softly. Gently.

"Feels that way," I say as I shift in my seat.

"Somehow you seem different."

"Really?" I ask, wrapping my arms tightly around my body.

What does he know? And what does he see? Because I don't see that. I just see me, exactly right now as I am. This. Not what I could be or what I might be capable of or that crappy thing that teachers always call potential.

"Well," he says, turning toward me, "you're here, aren't you?"

He leans in, warm and sweet, like a bakery at 5:00 A.M. His hair tickles its way across my forehead as he plants a light kiss there. I close my eyes with a sigh and a smile.

"You need to choose, Leah," Duffy breathes into my ear as he drags his lips lightly across my cheekbone. He rests his forehead against mine. "I won't be your second choice."

God, I didn't mean to cheat. Because this whole thing with Duffy, well, it just kind of happened. He just kind of happens. He shows up, and my blood runs hot, and like that, I am off course, spinning. He has never been part of the plan.

Eleven

"**Y**ou have got to be kidding me," I murmur as I make my way across the pool deck. It's been four full days since I skipped out of work and saw her last, but Valerie's fashion sense has not improved in the interim. Like some sunbather from the 1940s, she is sprawled out on an old blanket in a white halter suit and dark cat-eye sunglasses. I bet they are on loan from her grandmother, or the Smithsonian.

I watch her with a scornful smile as she closes her book, lifts her glasses with a raised pinkie, and looks over at me, trying to catch my eye as I pass by.

"Your friend Val," Troy says, stopping in front of me and lifting his stubbly golden chin toward Valerie, "she said you were sick last Friday."

He stretches his arms up, sticks his elbows out, and rests a battered-looking clipboard on the top of his head. He rocks back on his heels, essentially blocking my path with his excessive armpit hair. Gross.

"We covered for you," he says, mellow and a little too sweet, nodding at the gang of blond dudes staring down at us from the metal chairs ringing the perimeter of the pool, "no problem."

With a tight turn of my head I catch sight of Valerie, a couple of steps behind, books skipping along on her blanket, her chicken little legs straining under the effort, following me to my first chair.

"She's not my friend," I say to Troy. "She's just annoying."

I pull myself up into the chair next to the slide and turn around, feeling the baked metal rungs burning into my back as I slide down into my seat. I wish it weren't so hot. I exhale and watch a line of third graders jostle one another, climb the curved steps, then shoot down the slide, landing with sloppy splashes eight feet from my feet.

"Did you finish *The Tempest*?" Valerie asks later that afternoon, book under her arm, blanket in tow.

Her shadow, growing longer and longer as the day wears on, has been appearing next to mine about two minutes after I settle into each new chair.

She started out packing up her stuff each and every time, and then setting it all out again at her new location, but the last couple of times Troy blew a sharp blast on his whistle, she just dragged the whole shebang—books, blanket, and all—along the pool deck with me.

"I did."

I bubble up with excitement. I love *The Tempest*. I love anything with a good storm these days. Obviously.

I smile at her over my shoulder. "Did you?"

"Not quite." She holds up her book. Her bookmark is dangling, only about a quarter of the way deep.

"What do you think so far?" I ask, slowing for her answer.

"Leah!" a voice calls from outside the fence, and my heart races, caught, as I look past the XS board shorts and round grade-school bellies in tankinis to find Dani, fresh coppery streaks highlighting her auburn hair, her skin as brown as a dark Vuitton bag, walking toward the fence, waving at me. Len, our tiny blond pyramid topper, bounces along two steps behind her. Damn. I wave back, feeling defeated. I was hoping for Duffy.

"Tan enough?" I ask, stepping up my pace.

Dani rolls her eyes.

They have been gone practically all summer, staying with Dani's dad in Phoenix. My mother would never let me do something like that, even if she did get a divorce, which she would never do in a million years.

Dani laughs as I climb up onto my lifeguard chair. "It was *so* hot."

"Like an *oven*," Len confirms.

Her voice drifts away, her attention grabbed by

Valerie, pulling up next to me with her towel loaded, a little late to the party, as usual.

She parks herself in the corner between the fence and me, rolling out her blanket at the base of Len's and Dani's pedicured feet.

We all watch as she straightens her stack of books, angling them just so, and unfolds her body, leaning back against the fence. She stretches out her long, skinny legs, crosses her arms over her chest, and gives us a nod, letting us know that we now have her undivided attention. As if we even wanted it. God, she's not even picking up a book, or pretending to tan, or trying in any way to hide the fact that she is totally and completely earwigging on our conversation.

Tearing her eyes away from the spectacle that is Valerie, Dani says, "We saw Shane last night at the Keltie."

"Where were you?" Len asks teasingly. "He looked *so* lonely."

Right, like Shane could be lonely at the drive-in, surrounded by carhops in short skirts and unlimited hamburgers. Not possible.

"So we went over," Dani says.

"Just to say hi," Len says quickly as if I would be worried about their sliding into his backseat or something. I know Shane's not a cheater. That's my department.

"I've been so busy," I say, watching the water.

"Yeah? What have you been up to?" Dani asks.

Counting cars, I think.

"You know, not much," I say, making the understatement of the century or at least of my lifetime.

Valerie snickers.

"Wedding stuff?" Dani asks.

"Ooh, right," Len squeals. "Yorke is sooo lucky."

Valerie coughs and twitches against her blanket as she makes herself comfortable.

"Well," Dani says, drawing out the word, leaning back from the fence, scowling at Valerie.

Welcome to my summer, I think.

"We should go," she finally says, jabbing Len with a finger. "Tell Yorke I said congrats!"

"I will." Valerie chimes in, surprising Len and Dani even more than a pop quiz in algebra.

Their eyes say it all—they can't believe Valerie is invited to the social event of the season and they are not.

I lobbied hard to get my friends on the short list, but I was vetoed by Yorke, who wants no one too cute and tiny too close to her on her big day, and by my mother, who dislikes vegetarians and the difficulty they present to a caterer. Len is both.

"Me, too," Len says, unsure, waving at me as they both step back in unison, more than eager to get away.

Valerie waves at them distractedly, already reaching for the book at her side.

Dani and Len look at Valerie curiously and then at me, as if I had joined her secret club while they were gone for the summer. So not true.

"I'll call you," I say to them with a weak smile.

Dani nods, and then they turn their backs and walk away with their tan arms straight and stiff at their sides. I am so embarrassed.

"So . . . *The Tempest*?" Valerie asks, suddenly standing next to me.

I adjust my visor and get as comfortable as I can in my tall, sun-cooked chair. That ship has sunk.

"Really, Valerie," I say, my eyes scanning the crowded water, "don't bother."

I guess she doesn't know how this works, I think. She studies and studies and studies, and I don't even have to try. If I didn't dislike her so much at this moment, I would almost feel bad for her.

She adjusts the thing in her hair. Presses her lips together. Pulls at the thing in her hair. I can practically see the high-powered hamster on the wheel inside her head running faster and faster, trying to decide if I am referring to her incessant studying or her surprising poolside appearance as an old-time starlet.

"Don't do this," I say, my eyes on the water the whole time.

"What?"

"This." I point quickly from her to me, then back at her. "Talking." I sigh heavily and say, "Trying to pretend we're friends or whatever."

"Why?" she asks with an air of confusion.

"Why?" I huff in disbelief. Great. Now she is going to try to act as if she doesn't know what I am talking about. I know she is smarter than that, smarter than I am. She looks up at me, her eyebrows arching above the top of her curved glasses, curious.

"Seriously?" I ask incredulously.

"It's clear now why you never joined the debate team," she replies condescendingly. "Your proposition is definitely lacking."

Is it possible she isn't picking up on my evil vibes? I can feel them rolling off me in waves.

"The debate team is for myopics," I say, watching some kids dunk each other in the shallow end.

"I'm on the debate team," she says in a dry voice.

I know that.

She just continues to stand there at my feet, all teased hair and bewilderment, and I break down. Anger and frustration bubble over, and I smooth the tight ponytail on the top of my head, feeling my scalp prickle under the scorching sun. It's late summer. It's humid. I feel like I haven't drawn a deep breath since my mother laid down the law, restricting my movements and my life.

I haven't seen Duffy in days and days. Not since his ultimatum. No drive-bys, nothing. I feel as if somebody pulled the plug on the brightest thing in my life and I am fading fast.

There are boutonnieres, barrettes, and an endless stream of sandals to try on. Cap that off with a series of completely unnecessary ballroom dance lessons, and I am worn thin. Doesn't my family know I have bigger things to worry about? Like my cheating heart? I know it's down there somewhere, dragging along near the bottom of the simmering pool, below the kicking feet and the occasional swamped bug.

Throwing my hands toward her in frustration, I let it rip. "What do you want from me, Valerie? Other than to horn in on all my conversations and scare my friends away and stick your nose in my business at every opportunity and generally be as annoying as humanly possible?"

She takes a deep breath, adjusts her sliding

halter top around her pencil-thin neck, and looks over at her well-tended camp of books and lists and completed assignments.

"Well, maybe for once I'd like you to have to try," she says matter-of-factly.

My nose wrinkles up. "What does that have to do with anything?"

Across the length of the pool Troy is checking his watch, making sure that we are on schedule. He looks over, giving me and Valerie and our extended conversation a stern once-over.

"It has to do with *everything*," Valerie says, her head down as she fans the curled pages of Shakespeare back and forth in her hands.

The word USED, written in thick black marker along the face of the pages, appears, disappears, then appears again as if she is playing with a homemade flip book.

"Everything you've ever done," she says, steadying the book in her hands before looking up at me. "It all just falls into your lap."

That's right. I smile to myself.

"You don't have to try. Ever. Not even with Jon Duffy."

I suck in my breath at the mention of his name. That's what you think, screams through my brain, but I can't say it.

"Whatever." I hold my hand up, stopping her.

I'm done. I don't even want to know what she is talking about. I don't care. I stare out at the pool, my jaw tight, intent on saving a drowner.

Troy stands, tall and tan, and stretches for the sky. I hear the short blast of his whistle, and it's time to move on. I grab my water bottle and reach for my beach towel.

Valerie leans in, her red painted fingertips clinging onto my chair as she asks, "Do you realize how much it sucks to work this hard and always come in second? Always?"

I don't, obviously.

I look out, past the fence and the hills thick with trees, specks and flecks of yellow dandelions popping up through the green grass as it rolls out through the park and say coldly, "Lucky for me,

Valerie, my life is not one of your little second-place science experiments."

I hop down from the lifeguard chair and land lightly on the sizzling hot pavement right in front of her. I shrug my shoulders and flick my ponytail, intending to breeze right by her and make my way to the next chair, already warming itself for me in the bright sunshine.

But face-to-face, up close, her teased hair is melting in the sun and her red lipstick is worn away, feathering at the edges from that nervous habit she has of pressing her lips together, and I remember Valerie, small and smiling proudly, spelling bee runner-up year after year, perpetual class play understudy who never quite made it onto the stage even though her lines were perfectly memorized, even second chair in a morose clarinet quartet at Solo and Ensemble.

She's always been so smart, too smart for her own good. When we went to the science museum in second grade, we all had our lunches packed, sitting in our laps for the long and bumpy bus ride. The kids with neurotic parents like mine had juice boxes, both healthy and economical. The spoiled ones and the forgotten ones had soda. I was so jealous, an entire can of soda, wrapped in tinfoil to keep it cold.

Valerie gave a long, stuttering speech from the front seat about how the tinfoil wouldn't keep the soda cold. It would actually draw the cold out of the can. Probably something she thought we should all know since we were on our way to a science museum.

She sat alone for the rest of the ride. Didn't have a partner to climb inside the giant ear. Nobody shared a soda with her at lunch, and she posed for the souvenir photo inside a classic Model T by herself, even though she had her collar popped just like everybody else. She's never known when to stop.

"Move," I say to her impatiently. Right now the red ribbon winner is standing between me and where I want to go.

"I just want you to try for once," she says as she takes a step back, her heel landing right along the edge of the pool on the small white square marked 6FT, allowing me to pass, and I know this is about more than just Duffy or our failed grade school friendship.

"Try," she calls out, "fair and square." Her voice trails after me as I walk along the maze of beach towels and deck chairs.

Fair and square? My ears burn with embarrassment. Is she serious? Is she eighty? God, it would be so much easier to hate her if she weren't such a Girl Scout. Then I remember, of course, that she was. The girl is a minefield.

And even though you didn't have to wear the thing to school, just to the meetings, Valerie showed up in class at least once a week in her sad little green uniform. She had all the badges. They lined her vest and her sash, proving to the world that she was smart and helpful and could cook a pan of baked beans.

When I came home one day in third grade and announced that I wanted to join scouts, too, my mother, completely exasperated, said, "Really, Leah, nobody looks good in a green tam."

I feel condensation running lazily down my water bottle and dripping through my fingers. I don't turn back to look at Valerie, but I do consider, kind of frighteningly, that maybe my mother did know best. I haul myself up and take my place high above the tanning masses with a shaky smile.

Twelve

"Get me a skinny caramel macchiato," Yorke commands from the curvy little couch in the bridal salon as she twists her newly highlighted superblond hair up onto the top of her head. "Decaf!" she yells after my mother, who, even though Jinny the bridal shop lady offered to run out, is quickly disappearing down the flocked hall.

I am the only one who really needs this final dress fitting since I have the jugs to contend with. Freddie, of course, is a perfect size six. And Yorke made the surprising last-minute decision to wear our mother's wedding dress. It's a beautiful white silk gown, simple and elegant, with an empire waist and delicate beading at the hem and the neck. With just a few nips and tucks, it fit Yorke perfectly.

"A lovely tradition," Jinny coos as she helps Yorke step into the swirl of white silk puddling around her ankles behind the saloon-style doors of the large brides only dressing room.

"A necessity," I hear Freddie remark from behind the scrolled white door of her much tinier dressing room.

Swinging the dressing room door open with one hand, the sparkling hem of her dress trailing behind her, Yorke sweeps out into the main salon and pushes past me to step up onto the raised pedestal and stand in front of the gilded mirrors.

"Haven't seen Shane much lately," she says casually as she leans back so that Jinny can pin the long filmy veil into place at the crown of her head.

"Yeah," I say sharply while Zuska, the Slavic altering lady I have gotten to know too well, digs around in my armpits yet again, strategically placing the final pins.

I feel a little stab and could swear that Yorke picked a strapless dress just to spite me.

"There's a reason for that," I say into my armpit, feeling for the sharp offender.

I glance up with a dot of blood on my finger and find Yorke's expectant gaze on me in all three of the huge mirrors.

"I'm kind of over that," I say. And I am. Mentally I have broken up with him, over and over again. It's just that I haven't told him yet.

"Over what?" Freddie asks as she steps in front of the mirrors, her tiny, flat chest perfectly wrapped in satin.

"Over Shane," Yorke scoffs.

"Ri-ight." Freddie rolls her eyes at Yorke.

Watching them snickering together, I decide that maybe my dress might have taken a lot more work and that it still may be held together with a couple of straight pins, but it looks better on me. Definitely.

"I'm serious," I say.

"Come on . . ." Yorke chides as she turns to admire her side view, adjusting her uncooperative veil over one shoulder. "You and Shane´ are not breaking up."

"Who's breaking up?" my mother asks as she bustles in, snapping her cell phone shut and dropping it into her bag. An iced coffee and Yorke's caramel concoction are balanced in a recycled cardboard tray in her free hand. There's nothing for the nonbetrothed.

"Apparently Shane and Leah," Yorke says as she turns and reaches for the tray. "Yes!" she exclaims as she grabs at the coffee greedily and my mother backs off, ice rattling loudly when the cups slosh.

"Not officially," I say to Freddie quietly. "It's not official yet."

"Don't be silly," my mother says, swerving out of Yorke's reach. "Leah and Shane are not breaking up."

She sets the tray down, wedging it between the bridal magazines and the bounty of fresh flowers on the table. She straightens up to look at us. "They're fine." She smiles. "They're perfect."

My mother walks toward Yorke, head cocked to one side as she moves in. She lifts Yorke's veil expertly and lets it fall, slowly, so that it drifts down to settle over Yorke's shoulders. She passes behind Freddie, stops, and places one index finger on each shoulder, pulling back gently, making Freddie's bodice so tight the satin sings.

"Perfect," Freddie repeats to her reflection, almost silently.

My mother's hands graze across my shoulders when she steps behind me, lightly brushing over my fading tan lines and scuffed shoulder blade. I have been working hard, with a variety of bathing suits and a lot of self-tanner, to be strap mark free.

She smooths my hair back, adjusting it to fall over one shoulder, Chanel No. 5 filling my lungs as her eyes meet mine in the mirror.

"Your sister doesn't need any more stress right now," she stage whispers, and I droop under the weight of my dress. How can it be that the people who are supposed to love me the most are here, so close, all lined up shiny and promising, yet I feel so alone?

"She doesn't look stressed," I say, watching Yorke, sliding out of her dress behind the curved sofa.

"Don't be an idiot," Yorke says thickly, sipping the hot coffee and curling up on the satin settee in her underwear, her wedding dress in a ball at her feet. "I am totally stressed."

My mother lifts her brow at me before she reaches over to pick up Yorke's dress and heads off to find Jinny and a satin-covered hanger and protective bag.

"Why would you break up with Shane a couple of days before my wedding?" Yorke asks. "Are you retarded?"

She looks at me as if I am dumb enough to dignify that with an answer.

"He *has* to be there, Leah. Roger asked him to be an usher, for Christ's sake. What are you going to do about *that*?" She snaps a pink packet of sweetener before tearing it open. "And what about homecoming next year? And prom?" She rests the cup on her leg as she reaches for packet number two.

"What are you thinking?" she asks, shaking her head, pausing only to stir. "You're not breaking up." She dumps the last packet into her coffee and dismisses me, and the whole idea, with a wave of a brown stir stick and the turn of her head.

"You know what I think, though?" she says, looking over at Freddie with a dangerous grin. "You know who *should* be breaking up?" She rises slowly and saunters over to stand behind Freddie. We all know that according to the schedule, Evan should be gone by now. His time was up at the beginning of summer.

"Cut that boy loose already," Yorke says to Freddie's buttoned back. "I worry about you."

I watch her as she swirls the coffee stirrer around playfully in her tall cup, waiting for a reaction, her reflection clear in the two mirrors not blocked by Freddie. Her stomach is tight, the skin stretched across a tiny bulge, low but in the middle. Obvious now, but well hidden by her summer dresses and newly fitted wedding gown. My eyes are glued to it, my mouth open, my brain reeling, adding up the days and the months since Roger first appeared.

I step back, feet muffled in the thick cream carpet, eyes wide. I am not entirely surprised to find Freddie watching my reaction, nodding knowingly at me, because, like always, she knew but kept her mouth shut.

When we were really, really little, before we were good girls and had learned how to behave ourselves, our mother used to bribe us through boring things, like church, with the promise of candy.

"Whoever is quiet the longest gets a piece," she would say under her breath, holding her purse open a crack so we could peek inside and see the sweet prizes waiting for us there, knowing full well that Freddie could shut up forever if it was a competition.

Yorke would break down about halfway through the sermon and start whispering to whoever was unlucky enough to be sitting next to her, usually me, or humming to herself, sometimes even pinching Freddie in an attempt to get a rise out of her. It never worked. Freddie was so good that she even knew how to unwrap the candy that she had saved from the week before without a wrinkle of the wrapper, not so much as a rustle or a crinkle. She would sit back, feet swinging happily under the pew, a smug grin on her butterscotched lips.

"You know what I think?" Freddie says clearly, with a marked glance over her shoulder in Yorke's direction as she walks back to her dressing room. "I think you already have enough to worry about."

Well, I think, give that girl a sourball. Freddie wins again.

Thirteen

I don't think I've ever actually felt this way before. I am boiling over and betrayed, and I think I might be bitter. About Duffy, whose mom died and he could barely even be bothered to tell me. How come he didn't want to tell me? I guess he never did like me. He certainly never really trusted me.

And about Yorke, who managed to get pregnant *and* keep it a secret, a monumental feat for her, and Freddie, for faithfully, to the end, keeping her end of the bargain, even if that meant leaving me out.

Yorke and Freddie I can deal with, I have a lifetime of being last in line with them. But Duffy is fresh and new, the wound all mine, brewing and bubbling just under the surface of my skin.

"Just skim, Leah," Troy says, walking behind me with a padlock dangling from his finger as I stretch, reaching the long pole out over the well of the pool. "Don't stab and poke."

After we clean the pool, it takes me two tries to swing my leg up onto the first rung of my chair for my last night swim of the season. It's the second week of August, and the thought that this may be my last night swim ever, if my mother has her way, fills my veins with lead.

The pool has always been my place, separate from my sisters and my mother, a shimmering L-shaped space of chlorine and solitude. I hardly ever even get wet above the ankles, but at least it's all mine. And I don't want it to disappear, the way Duffy did.

I haven't seen him in forever. I have been avoiding Shane this whole time, but why bother if

Duffy is not even going to show up?

He said the choice was mine to make. Actually, I think his exact words were, "You need to choose, Leah," as he rested his head so softly against mine, but how the hell can I choose when he goes ahead and does it for me? Between him and my mother, it's as if I never even got the chance.

I hear the crack of a bat, and distant cheering fills the air. The smell of hot dogs sizzling on a grill drifts in on the breeze, then up and over the balcony of trees. A few parents float about in the sparsely populated pool, bobbing on the surface, lazy and relaxed. The little wild ones, the kids who usually fill the pool with shrieks and splashes, are across the road at the big park shelter, playing in a Little League tournament.

The sun is setting, and Troy turns on some classic rock. The first few notes, I think it's an old Boston song, bounce across the water and melt into me, loose and comfortable. I slip down, resting my head against the back of my chair, and spy Troy in the pool office, playing air guitar like a demon.

He sees me, smiles sheepishly, and finishes up with a wild riff and the thrashing of his guitar against the cinder-block walls. I clap silently and wave an invisible cell phone over my head in tribute to our swimming pool rock god. Troy bows, walks out of the office, and climbs back up into his chair, all business again.

The familiar sound of flipping pages snaps me back to reality. I flail my legs and knock my ankle against the sharp steel of my chair. I sit up straight, fully expecting to find Valerie coming at me, a piece of great literature in her hand, saying something stupid like "It's a great night to discuss verse," or "I find myself lost in a midsummer night's dream." But it's just a magazine that someone's left out on the deck, flipped open and rustling in the breeze.

I scan the perimeter of the pool, looking for a vintage bathing suit and skinny legs. It appears that Valerie is not here. I do a double take, because I can't fathom that she is not here, because this is the first time I have been at the pool, *all summer*, without Valerie at my side.

Nope. She is really not here. Hmm. She probably had to get those sunglasses and that halter suit back to the museum for carbon dating.

My brain lowers to a simmer. Without Valerie and her constant drone of facts and figures and historical statistics and plaguing questions, without that, for the first time in a long time, there is room in my head. I think I can actually think, but is that a good thing?

I know immediately, with a miserable slump of my entire body, that any vacancy in my brain right now is instantly going to fill with thoughts of Duffy or, more precisely, my lack of Duffy.

I flash forward to us together next year, dating, happy, and always on the move. We will be homecoming king and queen, because well, I'm me, and my mother and sisters all were homecoming queens before me. It's tradition. And Duffy will be king. We will ride along in the parade perched up on the back of a convertible, smiling and waving at the crowds lining the streets. Except that Duffy probably won't want to sit in the back and let somebody else drive.

And when we have our Friday night family

dinners at the club, will he park our car first and *then* come inside to sit beside me, his hair dark and wild in a blond sea of shining glaze and spray?

I bet I can make him fit the mold, chisel him down a bit, and wear away the rough edges. The thing is, though, I like the rough edges. They make me feel raw, tingling, and alive. And I like that.

The sun dips behind the tops of the trees, the lights come up softly under the surface of the water, and the swimmers appear to glow. I can hear chatter from the ball game. "Hey, batter, batter. . . . Hey batter, batter. . . ."

Another song comes on the radio, one I remember hearing the day that Duffy and I went to the river. It's slow at first, the guitar playing along quietly in the background, then it builds, thrumming with energy as we run toward the water, and suddenly it opens up, drums crashing, and the shock of the water hits us, cold and sharp, taking our breath away. A shiver runs down my spine when the song ends, the guitar trailing away, slipping off into the soft evening air like a metallic whisper.

I reach behind me, fumbling for the hooded sweatshirt I know is there, feeling for the softness. I pull it on, flipping my hair out over the hood and sliding the sleeves down over the tips of my fingers.

I resist the urge to pull the thick hood up over my head and think sad thoughts. What if I end up with no one? No Duffy, no Shane, and even no Valerie. At least when she's around, I have someone to talk to at the pool.

She doesn't bother me as much as she did in the beginning of the summer. I've built up my immunity. I am inoculated.

I guess there's always Troy, but he's never been much of a conversationalist. I watch him as the lights flicker to life around the fence line. His arms silently pound out the beat from the rock song on the radio, his knee bounces, toes working the bass drum, and I give up.

I stretch the sweatshirt out and around me, squeezing my knees into my chest, and build a tent. Arms wrapped tight, I rest my chin on my knees and gaze out over the nearly empty water.

A single swimmer glides silently by, lap after lap. A flutter of water follows him, then drifts away, absorbed by the surrounding stillness. It's as if he had never been there, never passed by. He's invisible, fleeting, a subtle shift, and then he's gone.

I watch him pass by again and squeeze myself tighter into my warm fleece world, determined not to let Duffy go, willing him to kick harder. I will not let him just drift away.

Why doesn't Duffy want to talk to me? Why did he disappear, poof, gone just as suddenly and mysteriously as he appeared? I thought he liked me, but I guess I was wrong. He never did. And I gave up everything for him—Shane, homecoming queen, guaranteed spot on the prom court, an easy senior year—all of it, gone, for nothing, and he can't even bother to drive by and wave. Well, I would have given up everything for him anyway. It's just that I never really got the chance to let him know.

"Last one out, pull the gate shut behind you," Troy calls out onto the dark, shadowy pool deck from inside the office. I'm the last one.

I'm packing up my stuff, and the night settles down quiet and still all around me. The ball games have ended. The families are driving off in minivans and SUVs, their headlights disappearing up the hill as they head for the Keltie to celebrate with ice cream sundaes and triple-stack burgers.

I pull the gate shut, hearing the metal latch clank tight behind me. The office light glows warm and soft, reflecting a shimmering square on the water. I look back, see Troy in his Devils swim jacket and tight red suit, the old office phone cradled to his ear, and give him a wave.

I hear the crackle of tires against gravel when I reach the end of the slope, the blacktop path cool and far less sticky at night. I clear the last of the trees at the bottom of the path, anxious to see who is picking me up. It's like the lottery, with my mother choosing the numbers. And Duffy's number never comes up.

I pause, momentarily caught in the headlights. Shit. She sent Shane.

My mother is the devil, and my life is like one of those kiddie rides at the amusement park. Sure, the car looks great, all shiny and bright, but you can't actually drive it. It's on a track. You just sit there like a dope and smile all big so your parents can wave and snap pictures. At first you might think you are going to get a chance at the wheel, but then you discover it doesn't even turn.

When you are little, it seems like fun, and maybe the hills you roll over feel big and scary and your stomach lifts a little bit each time. But now my stomach only sinks as I climb into Shane's idling car and his hand lands heavily on my thigh.

I press against the soft leather, and I know this car goes nowhere. No more diversions, no discoveries by dashboard light, no more dashing, from place to place, from car to car. I'm stuck.

Fourteen

"Now, you have everything?" my mother asks for the billionth time as she rifles through my bag, not trusting my packing abilities.

"Yes."

"Your dress, your shoes, all your . . ." She pauses to smooth out the lace underwear she has just refolded into a pink square. She stashes them along the side of the bag because apparently underwear doesn't belong where I put it, on top of everything else.

She looks up, eyes stopping for a second right on my boobs before she continues. "Underthings?"

Yorke and Frederique got the family names. I got the jugs.

She waits for an answer, as if I could somehow forget to wear a bra to my sister's wedding rehearsal. I haven't been out of the house without these things strapped in and hoisted since I was twelve years old. She knows that.

I lean my hip against the counter, cross my arms, and breathe, "Yes."

"I want to be sure. We can't overlook anything."

She digs through the entire bag again, down to the bottom.

"I can't believe you have to work today, of all days. You and your father," she huffs, flustered.

My dad is at work today, too. He left early this morning, having filled his travel mug full of hot coffee and driven off in his dew-covered truck well before the wedding insanity began.

"And you told them about the rehearsal?"

My mother seems to think there is a big

corporation running the public pool, not just Troy and his clipboard.

"Yes."

"You're sure?" She pauses again and raises her perfectly penciled brows, questioning the contents of my bag one last time as her fingers hover over the zipper, afraid to pull it shut and zip up her last chance to fret and worry.

Believe it or not, I have packed a bag before.

"Yes, it's all right there," I say with a confident nod.

She finally zips it shut, and I pull the polished round bamboo handles from her grip and hook them over my arm.

"I am putting the bag into your trunk on the right side, near your golf clubs, and hanging the dress, *in the plastic bag*, in the back on the passenger's side," I say, reciting the directions back to her exactly as they were dictated to me when she found me fifteen minutes ago standing in the kitchen and realized that she was on the hook to give me a ride to the pool for my afternoon shift.

"And don't, for any reason, get your hair wet."
My mother hovers behind me as we walk across the
foyer to the front door, car keys jangling from her
fingers, the quilted bag over my arm, backpack over
my other shoulder, dress, *in the bag*, swinging from
my fingertips.

"Even if somebody drowns!" Yorke yells over her
shoulder as she disappears up the stairs behind us
with rollers the size of soup cans in her hair. I pull
the door shut on her with a bang.

"I just don't know if this lifeguarding thing was
the best decision for you," my mother says as she
bears down on the gas, hooking into the park with a
sharp right. She looks over at me, eyes completely
unreadable under her dark Jackie O glasses. "I don't
know what you and your father were thinking."

I grip the seat, bracing myself for the descent
downhill, knowing no reply is necessary. My mother
is not the most attentive driver in the best of
situations, but one day before her first daughter's
wedding? Forget about it. We are a white gold blur,

whizzing past ten-speeds and strollers and dogs on the run.

"Did you talk to Shane today?" she asks.

"No." I sigh.

I know what she wants. I can feel her pressing down on me all the time. The nonstop pro-Shane propaganda is not really necessary.

She wants me to put on my pink blinders and follow the path that she has planned for me. She wants me to pretend I didn't see all those things and do all those things and *feel* all those things I felt with Duffy. Sometimes I wish I could. It would be so much easier.

"His tux should be ready," my mother says, her sharp tone competing with the *bing, bing, bing* of her turn signal. "Remind him to pick it up early tomorrow. Did you remember his corsage? Did Roger get him a gift?"

The questions pop in my direction like maternal machine-gun fire as she revs the engine and makes the final turn into the pool parking lot, angling randomly across four spots, scattering a gang of big boys on tiny bikes. They roll away like Skittles, glaring at us from under the brims of their baseball caps.

I push at the door.

"He may only be an usher," she continues, "but he is part of the wedding party after all. He'll sit next to you at the head table. It only makes sense."

I grab my bag and get out of the car.

"Someone will pick you up." My mother waves at me, not waiting for my response. She is already turning the car away, driving off, flipping her cell phone open as she zigs away.

I glance through the links of fence on my way toward the pool, hoping for a light crowd, an easy afternoon, and maybe even a chance that Duffy might be somewhere on the shady side, resting on some hood, waiting for me.

No such luck.

Most of the middle school is milling around outside the fence. Towels draped around their necks like prizefighters, they wait for the gates to swing open.

Heat shimmers, waves of it rising off the empty concrete deck as I grip my bag up against me and swim against the Coppertone-scented tide, pausing on my way past the kiddie pool to let two little girls with water running in little rivers down their backs pick their barefooted way across the blacktop path in front of me.

They pass by carefully, balancing on their tippy toes while I push past a knot of boys in board shorts with sporadically hairy upper lips. So totally thirteen. I can feel their eyes trailing me as I sneak in the side door marked STAFF ONLY in stenciled spray paint.

It's so different to be here during the day after working a calm, quiet night shift. The water glares at me in the afternoon sun, blinding and bright. White caulk fills the cracks on the deck. It oozes up, warm and soft, like marshmallow filling in a concrete Pop-Tart.

Valerie is outside the gate, her skinny legs poking through the slit in a saffron sarong that could almost be in style if it didn't look like it came straight from the Goodwill.

She is sitting with her usual perfect posture, her legs crossed at the ankles. She looks expectant, but not in a Yorke kind of way. I watch her licking at a melting Drumstick, the paper wrapper, next to her on the concrete, neatly folded like origami, and I am struck by her stillness. She looks almost beautiful from here, in a bony, brown-haired, bookish kind of way.

Watching the clock over the office doorway, I swing myself into my chair. It is the exact same clock that hangs next to the flag in each and every classroom in my school.

I sit and stare at it ticking for a few seconds, enjoying the irony that this same clock is the one we stare at desperately for three seasons of the year. All day from eight to three, we will it to tick faster and run down the school day as quickly as possible. Here it silently steals summer away in splashes and seconds.

It clicks to one o'clock.

Then Troy blows the whistle, long and hard, and unleashes the frenzy. Valerie walks in, three minutes later, with her blanket and overworked tote bag, and settles in next to me. I watch her spread out, and my equilibrium, temporarily shaken last night with her unexpected absence, returns to normal.

"You know Mr. Ridley?" Valerie asks out of the blue sometime that afternoon. She stops reading and props open the encyclopedia she is skimming.

Her sunglasses—not the cat-eye ones from before, these are rounder—perch on the end of her nose. She looks over the top of them to see if she has my attention.

"The one with the Porsche?" she prompts.

Oh, yes, I know that Porsche.

"Yeah?" I ask, my eyes on the clock again, wondering where this is going.

"Well, it seems that Mr. Ridley was working out at the gym at the club, your club, you know, lifting weights, doing lifts or dead squats or whatever they're called."

Dead lifts. Shane does them for football.

"What are you talking about?" is right there, rudely on the tip of my tongue, but I stop myself.

"Well," she pauses dramatically. "The whole front of that gym is glass, a huge window, you know." She looks at me, and I nod. "So, Mr. Ridley is lifting," she pantomimes lifting a heavy bar over her head, her arms actually straining under the imaginary weight, "when all of a sudden, right in front of him, you know how it is," she pauses again, "his Porsche goes squealing by. And he's not in it."

"Oh, no."

"Oh, yes. It just drives off. Racing toward the lake. Good-bye," she says, squinting and waving into the distance.

She leans back against the fence, and I wait for her to adjust herself. When she's sure she's comfortable, obviously enjoying my frustrated interest, she continues.

"And the whole time the Porsche is driving away, it's supposed to be in the back lot at the club getting washed and detailed, but somehow it's absolutely roaring down the lake road." She scoots herself forward. "Or so I heard."

I imagine the Porsche, the spoiler lifting as it

gains speed, popping over the little hills that dot the golf course.

"So what happened?"

"Oh," she says, her voice muffled as she tucks her head under her arm and reaches over to grab the book she was reading when she started the story, "he dropped the weights." Looking down, she continues. "Heard he broke his toe." She drops the heavy book into her bag with a thick thud. "Threatened to sue the club."

Troy taps at his watch, looking over his shoulder to be sure the clock on the wall is right. It's 4:59. He looks around at every chair, catching the attention of each lifeguard with a small lift of his chin, and I stand, distractedly, wanting Valerie to finish the story before the commotion of closing time begins. I know that she is toying with me, that she knows what I want to know.

"And?" I ask urgently.

"Oh, and Jon Duffy got busted," she says, stopping her book packing long enough to make annoying air quotes around the word "busted."

Troy blasts his whistle and catches me completely by surprise. I try to exhale, but all my air is gone, my lungs empty as my head fills with the tinny shrill of the pool at closing time. My whistle drops from my lips.

Valerie walks over to me and slings her bag at the base of my chair. It knocks up against the metal leg with a clunk. I look at her, my eyes glazed, unable to focus.

I know in my heart that Valerie is trying to redeem herself. It's in the way she leans forward, looking up at me beseechingly, talking urgently and as privately as possible in this public place as the crowd mills around us, shouting and waving to one another, making plans and saying good-byes.

"So," she continues, resting her elbow on the platform near my ankles, "Big Duff worked a deal. Jon Duffy can still park cars at the club, but he can drive them no farther than the painted lines at the edge of the lot."

She rises up onto her tippy toes, motioning me to come closer.

She whispers into my ear, "I'm sure he doesn't like to talk about it." She settles back on her heels and says, "But he's probably grounded for the rest of his life."

My brain is buzzing. Reeling. I sit back down stunned. God, do you know what this means? He didn't disappear. I didn't get dumped. He just drove off in the wrong car.

I look over at Valerie, realization dawning in my eyes.

She smiles up at me, then reaches down to grab her bag.

She pauses. Breathes in.

"Are you going to get him back?" she asks shyly, and I realize that she is not being petty or vindictive.

She is being genuine and true, and unlike everybody else in my life, the ones who think they know exactly what they are going to get, Valerie might actually expect something more from me. She's raising the bar.

"I'm gonna try," I say, and she smiles at me, bold and bright.

The fence shakes behind me, jarring me back to the present tense.

"You call this a job?" Yorke's voice chides, and I jump, twisting in my chair, surprised to find both my sisters, overdressed for almost any occasion in short summer dresses and high-heeled sandals, standing on the worn grass under the smokers' tree.

I scramble down from my chair to face them, and Valerie scurries out of the way, like a bug. She hovers about three feet away but doesn't leave.

"I can't believe you're here," I say to Yorke.

"Neither can I," she replies coolly, lifting her sunglasses to stare at Valerie, giving her the look of death.

Valerie stammers without saying a word and stoops to pick up her stuff. She crosses between me and Yorke and Freddie with her eyes locked on mine. I stand stock-still and watch her go, silently trying to stop her.

I am torn, hating and loving Valerie, desperate to chase after her and dig for details, and dying to get away, to ditch my sisters and find Duffy. She can't just drop a bombshell like that and then walk away. I can't decide if I want to vomit or knock her teeth out.

"I had to get out of the house," Yorke says, her eyes following Valerie. "Roger is driving me insane." She looks over at me with a pained look on her face. "Literally insane."

"Or figuratively," Freddie adds. "What was that all about?"

"What is *she* all about?" Yorke sniffs with a flick of her long blond hair. Valerie's shoulders crawl up around her ears protectively, and she stops, hunched, and gives the three of us one last look before disappearing into the girls' dressing room.

I don't answer.

I am ashamed that my sisters see only the worn swimsuit and the bony shoulders, the wrong color toenail polish and the less than perfect smile. They don't notice that her slight overbite hides an awesome laugh and that Valerie's brain might be even bigger than Freddie's.

I start to unwind the heavy green hose from the fence.

Yorke rolls her wide eyes and asks impatiently, "Can we go?"

"You're early," I say, with a nod toward the clock hanging over the office. A little gurgle of warm water leaks from the tip of the hose. "I've still got work to do."

Yorke cocks her hip and crosses her arms. Her toe taps up a little puff of dust. She is evidently displeased with the idea of waiting.

"Is that your boss?" Freddie asks, lifting her chin toward Troy and the office.

I nod, looking at the sign propped in the corner of the office window that says WE DON'T SWIM IN YOUR TOILET. DON'T PEE IN OUR POOL.

"Whoever he is, he'd better not make me late," Yorke says, acting like she doesn't even know Troy, like that one year of college she's got under her belt somehow wiped her memory clean.

It's tragic, since Troy and Yorke were in the same class. They probably napped next to each other in kindergarten or shared a knuckle-bending slow dance in the middle school gymnasium. Probably passed each other in the halls every day.

Yorke and Freddie do not acknowledge his presence in any way. My sisters stand shoulder to shoulder on the far side of the fence, watching him from a distance, their designer sunglasses not quite large enough or dark enough to hide their indifference.

"Just go," I say, the heavy hose drooping in my hand, the weight of the words I wish I could say sitting like lead in my mouth.

Freddie backs away, her face surprised.

"Fine," Yorke says, with a dramatic shove from the fence. "You can find your own way for once."

"Fine," I say, bolder than she is for the first time, breathing deep, full of myself, till they do turn and walk away. With a trailing wave from Freddie, I feel my shoulders start to shake.

"I got it. I got it."

Troy's bare feet are slapping toward me. He looks troubled, something I didn't know he knew how to be.

"I got it," he says again as he jogs up next to me and takes the hose from my hand.

I think maybe this is the only thing he can think of to say, that maybe his brain is stuck on *repeat*, that he is stunned senseless by the sight of me tearing up.

We both stop and stare at Yorke's car rolling off down the road. He must have seen the whole thing.

I walk over to my chair to collect my stuff, shaking my head because I don't know what he thinks of me. Well, actually I do. He thinks I am just like them.

"Thanks, Troy," I finally stumble and say.

He smiles, and I feel slightly forgiven as the cool spray from his hose dances across my toes as I go.

"Will you help me?"

The car door is already swinging shut when I catch up with her. I stand, alone in the grass, knowing that the girl who has spent the summer trying to trump me is the only one I can trust.

She turns and asks, "Help you try?"

I nod.

Her eyes light up, and I open the passenger door open and slide into a worn bucket seat.

"What exactly did you have in mind?" Valerie asks as she rattles the engine to life.

"Find Duffy," I say, staring straight ahead as we rumble out onto the street. It's that simple.

"A quest," Valerie says excitedly, grinding the gears.

I can live with that.

"I have things to say," I explain.

"You will not just be noble in thought but in action." Valerie lays it on thick as we leave the park.

Sure, I think, trying to see past the petrified bug remains on the windshield. But she's right.

We try the minimart first, then the Gas n Go, followed by Fosdal's bakery on Main Street, basically any place that sparkles with sugar, spots that Duffy frequents for sweet fixes and gallons of juice. At the corner I consider trying the auto parts store, knowing it is a stretch, but my knowledge of his life outside the confines of a car is pretty limited.

"What are we looking for?" Valerie asks, her eyes scanning the street.

The light changes. I realize we have it all wrong. There is only one place he can be.

"Head for the club," I say, certain, as Valerie floors it and we head for the highway.

Valerie's VW shakes and shimmies at anything over sixty. You can't hear the radio or the road or the books dancing on the backseat, only squeaks and metal and the engine bearing down.

"Is this top speed?" I ask, watching the gearshift wiggle between us.

"It is the people's car," Valerie answers haughtily as she turns onto the lake road.

"Well, tell the people to step on it," I say, ignoring the buzz of my phone for the five hundredth time. My sisters have obviously made it to the church, and my mother is in panic mode.

The parking lot at the club is pretty empty. A few cars sit in the sun, but it's too late for a good tee time and too early yet for dinner.

When we shudder to a stop on the parking pad, a black-haired valet, an older man I think I recognize, pauses, his tan hand outstretched, unsure if he should open the door or send us around to the back.

He leans down and looks in the open window.

"Is Jon Duffy here?" I ask, and he smiles, happy to see someone blond and parkable.

"No, no, Miss Johnson, not yet."

I flop back, and his smile falters.

"I think he's here later," he says, "parking for dinner."

Somehow I am too late and too soon all at the same time. Valerie looks over at me, and I shrug.

"Thanks." Valerie waves to the valet, and she circles back through the parking lot.

"Where to?" she asks, scooping her sarong between her knees to shift into second.

"I have no idea," I say.

"We can't stop now," Valerie says, chugging back

down the driveway, away from the club. "We just got started."

I admire her spirit. Not in a glee club kind of way, but in a damn, you're going to get up and go again kind of way. I don't know where that comes from. I want to crawl under a rock and die.

"Give me a break," I say, slumping into my seat, watching the countryside speeding by, at least as fast as this car allows it, and sigh. "I'm just a beginner."

"What about his house?" Valerie asks optimistically.

"Sure." I nod, ready for the next turn.

She slows. "Do you know where it is?"

"No. Do you?"

"No."

"But you know everything," I say.

Valerie rolls her eyes at me.

"You really don't know where he lives?" she asks.

She's assuming that Duffy and I had some kind of normal relationship, with dinner dates and long phone calls and good-night kisses at the front door.

I sigh, mentally scolding myself for using the past tense.

"He lives at Big Duff's house."

"Which is where?"

I shrug, my shoulders heavy. I was hoping and hoping, and now I am hopeless. No matter how much I want to keep going, to change what has already happened, to say what should have been said, my mother is waiting. There is always that.

"Just take me to the church," I say.

Valerie nods and cranks a left.

It's quiet as we pull up in front of the church, the quiet that a summer evening gets when everyone is sitting down to dinner, when the sun hits one last high note, lighting the world up in gold. We sit for a second and soak it in.

I climb out and pull my bag from the back-seat.

"There's always tomorrow," Valerie sings.

And I laugh a little to make her feel good.

I let the door fall shut, the weight of it taking care of most of the work.

"I'll see you then," I say.

Valerie smiles at me and then putters away.

Fifteen

The church is half decorated. Okay, make that three-quarters, since everything is here but the flowers. They will arrive tomorrow morning, bundles of pink blooms, fresh, right before the ceremony. The white silk bunting, draped across every pew and every polished railing, glows in the kaleidoscope of light that slants in through the stained glass windows lining both sides of the nave.

The altar has a shiny pink satin runner on the steps, and tall, thick candles with Y 'n' R monograms stand at the ready, waiting to be lit with long, tapered matches. And I missed it all.

Instead of being here, decorating and making my mother happy, I have been making my way through the countryside with the smartest girl in town, foolishly letting myself believe, chasing after a boy who probably doesn't even want to be found. I tried. I failed. I'm doomed.

I slip down the stairs, heading for the ladies' room in the church basement to change into my wrinkle-free dress. I hit the first step with a sniff. It smells just the way our church always does, like old ladies. Why do church basements always smell like someone's grandma? And no, I don't mean my grandma. She wears Guerlain. This smells more like stale coffee and brittle bones.

I hustle, speed dressing in the cramped stall, and climb up the back stairs that lead directly to the altar, using the secret pathway that my sisters and I discovered during hours of droning services and years of boring after-school religious ed.

I walk silently along the gleaming altar, facing

the rows and rows of empty wooden pews that will be filled tomorrow afternoon with misty-eyed ladies and dark-suited gentlemen. Pretty much anyone who ever met my parents will be here to watch Roger and Yorke say I do.

My mother slides in close to me as soon as I reach the aisle, grabs my arm, and takes me aside like a child, maneuvering me into an apse, away from Roger's manicured family, her fingers tight and white on my shoulder.

"So happy you could grace us with your presence," she breathes into my ear just as Shane walks through the doors, right on time for the rehearsal, filling my stomach with a mixture of dread and relief.

"Why is he here?" I hiss at my mother, twisting out from under her hold, regretting the words as soon as they leave my lips.

"Roger invited him," my mother whispers discreetly, hiding her words behind her hand.

I huff, blowing a stray hair away from my face.

It's not like he needs to be here. He's just an

usher, for God's sake. Do you really need to rehearse leading great-aunts and real estate agents to their seats? I'm pretty sure you just tuck their fingers safely into the crook of your thick biceps and drag them along to the next available pew. Done. No practice necessary.

"Shush." She scolds me almost silently over her shoulder, not wanting to draw attention to our disagreement.

"Do not embarrass me, Leah," she says, her smile thin and dangerous.

She tilts her head, waiting for my acquiescence. I am a dust mite, so tiny, so powerless, her breath could blow me away.

A prism of light, brighter than any of the colors streaming through the stained glass windows on each side of the church, winks at me. It's Yorke's huge engagement diamond flashing in the sunlight from across the altar. I nod and take my place in the bridal lineup, avoiding Shane's eyes.

Reverting to old dance lesson habits, I move through the rehearsal without really trying, my eyes always on Freddie, shadowing her, the same moves, the same expressions, and the same silence.

I always knew I hated Roger.

The cars creep along the drive to the club in the blaze of a summer sunset. Shane and I are last, slowly winding our way from the wedding rehearsal at the church, through town, to the rehearsal dinner. We are the ass end of a parade of luxury vehicles, crawling, one at a time, to unload at the club's doorstep. The valet is still a small silhouette against the burning backdrop.

My left leg is numb under the pressure of Shane's state championship spiral grip. I keep my eyes trained on the club, watching for a glimpse of Duffy, seeing Yorke up ahead, getting out of Roger's red car, seeing the bristle of Roger's hair by the driver's door as he gives excessive and intricate instructions to the valet on proper parking procedure.

My eyes are open wide, flicking from side to side, from scene to scene, never really focusing, trying to keep up with my brain as it clips along.

A blur of summer smells, sounds, and sights, the ones you can experience only while cruising along in a convertible, blast up against my body. I'm alert, running on all cylinders, hoping to see Duffy somewhere, anywhere. I'm gunning for one more chance.

I'm sure he hasn't given up on me completely. I'm sure the real reason he hasn't shown up in so long is because he couldn't. He has been grounded. Just like Valerie said. He's still willing. He's just . . . carless.

I breathe a big sigh of relief and blow the last of the stale church air from my lungs. It's no wonder I haven't seen him. He hasn't had a car. He couldn't find me. But I think, squinting into the glare of the silver Benz right in front of us, from what I remember, the boy does have legs.

My fingers tap nervously on the buff leather armrest, tense, each revolution of Shane's flashy rims bringing me closer and closer to my destiny.

I have a perfect view of the lake, the club, the fairways. Big Duff is out on the course in some very fancy brown and white spectator golf cleats. He is getting into a cart, heading out to the ninth hole with some woman about my mother's age.

I watch, my eyes hungry and hopeful, as they laugh and she flicks her highlighted hair around, obviously enjoying Big Duff's jokes. I sink down in my seat, dreading that Duffy might be out there, too, on the rolling green course, driving around like his dad, but in a much larger car, with a much younger girl.

My brain is a little gob of matter that rattles around in my skull when we jerk to a stop, stalling a couple of car lengths from the front door.

Roger's relatives are tumbling from a gold Cadillac like clowns at the circus. They just keep coming and coming, some with hair just as red and just as big as any real clown. All they need are those big, floppy clown shoes to slow down this processional even more.

I crick my neck, trying to see past them and their big hair.

"I am so *hot*," I say, cranking the AC in the open

car, tugging at the vent in front of me, redirecting its flow, pulling on my visor to block the setting sun.

"You got that right," Shane says all low and sexy.

I scowl at him, but I am not really paying attention. I am flopping around impatiently, heavy in my low-slung seat, my eyes skimming over the leather of the dash, dreading the moment the door opens and Duffy is there, standing next to me, and wishing it were right now. Suddenly Shane leans in, taking advantage of the momentary lull, and starts just totally letching all over me. His hands, his eyes, his lips, they're everywhere, rubbing up against me, pulling on my dress, flicking across my skin.

"Come on," he says, sliding one hand along my thigh and under the hem of my dress, his breath steaming into my face.

I push him off, anger shooting straight through me from the top of my head down to my toes. I pinch my legs together and lock my knees. This is officially hell on wheels.

"Yorke and Freddie do it," Shane says with a pout, inching the car forward.

Disgusted, I lift my brows at him.

He shrugs. "Boys talk."

"Pointing out the sluttiness of my sisters is not the way to get into my pants."

"What is then?" he asks, dropping the car into park with a lurch as we finally pull up to the base of the curved steps.

"Shane," I say, kicking the door open with my sandaled foot, leaving a big smudge mark on the soft leather panel, "you're such an asshole."

I don't wait for a valet or for Duffy or for anyone to hold the door open and help me. I want out.

Somebody does appear, though, a red jacket blurring behind me as I stalk off, the light brush of fingertips grazing against mine as I step away and stride up the stairs away from Shane, feeling, or maybe just imagining, a luminous trail of electricity tingling on my skin.

I find him, hours later, standing in the shadows of the old barn that is used as the club's garage. Full of tractor mowers and golf course equipment, it is hidden away from the main building behind some tall trees at the back of the parking lot.

There's an old wooden kitchen table on the concrete slab just inside the massive sliding door. The black-haired valet from earlier and a couple of other guys are sitting around in the dim light on mismatched chairs, elbows on the scratched surface, playing gin with a beat-up deck of cards.

A board is nailed to the wall over a workbench behind the table, numbered car keys hanging from tenpenny nails. A red jacket hangs loosely on the back of one of the empty chairs at the table.

The loud clack of my heels across the pavement draws attention away from the game as I walk toward the barn, but at least it drowns out the wild thumping of my heart. I stop short of the doorway when I see Duffy standing outside, partially hidden in the shadow of the roof.

He steps toward me, hands crammed deep into his pockets.

"Why didn't you tell me?" I blurt out.

I have waited for this moment for too long, and

it comes out in a rush, before I am ready to say it.

"Tell you what?" he asks, his voice and his eyes as flat as lake water on a cold early morning.

"About Mr. Ridley's Porsche, about getting caught. About why I never see you anymore," I whisper.

About everything, I think, as I pause for a second to catch up with my thoughts, the list continuing in my head, a desperate rambling too embarrassing ever to be spoken out loud. I want to know everything. Everything about you. I want to know that you liked me, that you were actually interested in me, that I meant something to you. I want to know that I didn't screw everything up for us.

"Why didn't you tell me about your boyfriend?" Duffy asks, lifting his chin toward the parking lot, where Shane and Roger are now stumbling, drunk and loud toward Shane's car, its white paint gleaming under the glow of a lamppost.

I can see Shane reaching into the open passenger side and digging around. I watch as he stands and then sloppily bumps knuckles with Roger, leaving me feeling queasy and embarrassed. Roger lights what looks like two cigars, and the smoke from the burning embers curls up, chasing away the summer bugs circling the buzzing lamp over their heads.

"That was nothing," I say, dismissing Shane, but glad to be hidden away under the cover of darkness.

"Then what was I?" Duffy asks.

His eyes glitter green and angry as he steps out of the shadows.

"What were you?" I ask, steam building behind my words. "You were the guy that stopped showing up, that pretended that he liked me and then disappeared. You were the guy that left me waiting and wondering, the guy that never told me what happened. I had to hear it all from Valerie Dickens, the girl that gets most of her information from old library books and the forensics club. At least I didn't tell Valerie to tell your dad to tell you that I had a boyfriend. That's so seventh grade."

"No, you let me see it in action. That's *so* much better."

"I didn't want that to happen." I fumble. "That wasn't my choice."

"Neither was I apparently," Duffy says solemnly, his hands out in front of him, stopping my approach, his eyes searing into mine.

He drops his hands, silent, and then turns and slips away, up the slope toward the golf course and into the dark night. He doesn't look back.

I take a few steps and sag down onto the thick green grass, my shoulders hunched up, a sob stuck in my throat.

"Let him go, Leah." My mother's voice splinters down my spine.

I turn, twisting toward her, stunned to find her there, half hidden in the darkness under the trees.

"Broken hearts can always mend," she says, walking toward me slowly, and I wonder how much she has heard, how much she knows, and why she sounds like an old love song, fuzzy but somehow recognizable.

"What do you know about it?" I say as I stand, not trusting the warmth in her voice, testing it for the edge.

"More than you realize."

"Sure," I scoff.

"I do," she insists. "I just want what's best for you."

"Maybe you don't know what that is," I say.

I am suffocating and crawling out of my skin, desperate to chase after Duffy, to have him back, to have that part of my life back, right here and right now, but I am nailed to the spot.

"Maybe it's him," I say.

"It's not," she says simply, as if there were no doubt.

She looks at me, slightly exasperated but with patience.

"Let me live my own life," I say without thinking.

"I do," she says softly, taking another step toward me. "And you have a perfect life."

"No, I don't." I shake my head. I back up, fists clenched at my sides. "I have Freddie's life and Yorke's life and yours, too. None of it is really mine. And none of it is perfect. At least not for me."

She nods along with me, raising an eyebrow, like she wants to pretend to understand what I am talking about. I know she doesn't.

"Why don't you want more for me? Why don't I

get anything different, anything that's just for me?" I ask, years of frustration coming out in a ragged, defiant rush.

She tilts her head, tensing up. "Like what?" she asks, crossing her arms across her chest, a flash of anger flaring in her voice.

"Like him," I say, plunging forward, ignoring the signs pointing toward disaster. *Danger. Beyond here be dragons.*

She breathes out and speaks slowly and clearly. "He's the hired help, Leah. He's a mistake."

"Well, then," I counter, "let me make my own mistakes."

"You don't know what you are asking." She sighs, sounding weary and unexpectedly wise. "You don't realize the mistakes you can make at your age."

"Like Yorke?" I ask quietly, bringing up the forbidden topic, feeling suddenly daring and fearless here in the darkness with a broken heart.

"Yes, Leah," she says heavily, rubbing her forehead, the bracelets making a slow, soft *shink, shink, shink* as she moves. "Like Yorke."

Sixteen

"Where is the pink one?" the pinched-looking photographer mutters as he trips into the bright flower-filled dressing room, white socks peeking out from under his dark, wrinkled suit pants. He is moving at breakneck speed, trying to capture the multitude of candid shots that Yorke wants as a reminder of this blessed event.

"Where's the pink one?" he says again, almost shouting this time, sounding frantic, adjusting the thick black camera strap around his neck as his eyes stop on each of my sisters, apparently unable to tell us apart.

You would think the fact that one of us is wearing a wedding dress would at least give him a place to start, but he looks lost and flustered, not up to the process of elimination. I hold up my pink bouquet to help him out.

The bouquets are a compromise that Yorke begrudgingly accepted, a way to include my mother's favorite color scheme, somehow, in the all-pink wedding. My bouquet is a combo of light pink and white tea roses tied with a dangling satin pink ribbon. Freddie has yellow daisies and white tea roses with a yellow ribbon, and Yorke, a massive bunch of white lilies bound with a thick baby blue ribbon.

The photographer snaps his fingers above his head to get my attention, as if I am a dog or a small child. He clicks away, repeating the words *and soft smile, and soft smile*, a madman with his finger on the trigger as I pose with a strained smile on my lips, not feeling soft at all.

I turn back to the oval mirror on top of the dressing table. I want to curl up and let this day slip by, but every time I close my eyes I see Duffy walking away from me, fading into the distance until I can't separate tan skin from dark sky.

Riding home late last night with my sisters, after everyone else had gone, after all the drinks were drunk and all the toasts toasted, I balled myself up tight in the backseat, Duffy's voice crushing me.

Fog floated over the surface of the lake as our tires hummed along on the damp asphalt. Willowy branches brushed up against the car on the tight lake road. The piers and docks reached out into the dark water like wooden fingers. I hoped we would somehow lose our way or at least lose control and crash into the water, swamping Yorke's secret and Freddie's silence, so I could slip away from everything and everyone and slowly sink to the bottom, light as a feather, heavy as a rock, because it turned out he never did like me. I was right. That's it. The spell is broken. No sparks, no heat, no rush.

Pressing my forehead against the cool dressing

room mirror, I feel my skin wrinkling up, my bones turning to dust, my blood leeching right out of me. My life is over.

"It's time," the photographer announces, and I look up to see his snapping fingers hovering in the open doorway, his body already out in the vestibule, on the move.

I gather up my bouquet and take one last look in the mirror. I pinch my cheeks, then give up and follow Freddie out into the church entrance.

The candles have been lit, there are flowers everywhere, and the pink satin runner has been laid out along the length of the center aisle now that all the guests have been seated.

My mother, long ago escorted to her first-class seat at the front of the church by Shane in his tuxedo, waves to us over the sea of whispering cousins and family friends, any harsh feelings or retribution from the night before temporarily silenced by the emotion of the day.

I get a glimpse of Betty, our plump pipe organist, fanning herself and the stations of the cross with one of the custom-designed wedding programs. She will wobble along until the three harp players, who are playing softly and beautifully from the balcony above, break into the wedding march at the first sight of Yorke.

Freddie and I line up, yellow and pink bouquets at the ready. I am right in front of the closed double doors. First out of the gate, for once, my cue is the opening notes of Handel's "Largo."

My dad stops pacing out front on the church lawn and sweeps up the steps with a broad smile on his face. He wraps me and then Freddie in a tight, wistful hug that smells of fresh air and sweet cologne.

Wiping at his eyes, he says to us, "I've got something to show you," and he reaches into the hidden chest pocket of his black tuxedo jacket and takes out an overstuffed silver money clip and a small wallet-size photograph that is frayed at the edges.

Leaning in, I see my parents, in miniature, on their wedding day. My dad's hair is so dark. The smile lines that I love around his eyes are not smiled into yet. My mother looks so young, younger than Yorke does right this minute as she dawdles in the bride's dressing room, determined to keep the world waiting for as long as possible.

"Yorke looks just like your mother did on our big day," my dad says, beaming.

It is amazing. They look like twins, or at least like sisters, except my mother had an eighties-looking beaded headpiece and some dark Madonna-ish eyeliner that Yorke would never stomach.

Freddie's eyes flicker from the photograph onto mine. I look again. I recognize the thickness of my mother's shape and the slight swell straining the empire waist of her dress. Freddie steps back behind me, taking her place in line.

"Just last week it was twenty-two years," my dad remarks with a note of awe in his voice. He slips the photo back into his suit coat and tugs at the hem, smoothing everything out, readying himself for his trip down the aisle. "Can you believe it?" he asks me before he retreats into the dressing room to get Yorke.

I can't. They were married in August. Yorke was born in January. I'm subtracting, quickly doing the math in my head as the first few notes of "Largo" drift under the door.

I twist, my pink flowers bobbing out in front of me at an awkward angle, as I ask Freddie frantically, "So, Mom—"

"God," Freddie interrupts with a nonchalant roll of her eyes as the doors swing open and I turn myself back toward the swelling music, "you always did suck at math."

The photographer's huge flash sears my eyes with a bright pop, scorching me to the spot. I hesitate, blinded. Freddie nudges me with her pee-yellow bouquet, and I take my first couple of step-togethers down the pink satin aisle on shaky legs. I am nothing but swimming spots and a fake smile.

I keep blinking, trying to bring things into focus. Like the little anniversary celebration my parents had last week around the kitchen table. Blowing out the candles on my dad's favorite three-tiered chocolate cake, 22 written across the top in thick buttercream frosting. My mother had joked, as she sliced the cake, that Yorke should be glad. Roger would always have a reminder of his wedding anniversary since it was so close to theirs. "And," my mother had laughed, frosting clinging to the tips of her fingers as she showed off her new sapphire anniversary band, "your father is well trained."

Or the wedding photo on the mantel in the sitting area of my parents' bedroom. It's the only one that I know of in our entire house. It's a glossy eight-by-ten in a curved silver frame, a close-up of their smiling young faces and nothing else.

I guess I always thought that Yorke just popped out early, eager to crash the party as always. It's one of those things you know in the back of your mind, but you don't want to believe, like there are bits of bug in every bite of your peanut butter, that Christopher Columbus could have cared less if the world was round, or that your mother was a little loose and had to get married.

Somehow I make it to the altar, not sure that I even once touched the ground on the way, and take my place, turning toward the crowd. As Freddie takes her last few measured steps, I glance out over our assembled friends and family who are shifting impatiently in their seats, waiting for Yorke's imminent appearance.

I focus on the halo dancing around the candle burning next to me and breathe small, shallow breaths, amazed at how a huge space like this, filled with almost everyone you love, can feel so tight and narrow. I wonder how many of them were here to witness the last time this same dress took the trip down this same aisle under almost the exact same circumstances.

I am dizzy with disappointment. With my parents, my sisters, and myself for thinking and believing that their way was the only way. I know now that this isn't true love or perfection or happily ever after. It's not even meant to be. This is a broken condom at the end of a drunken night. This is a generational walk of shame with two hundred spectators.

The wedding march floods the church, and Yorke appears at the door—the perfect bride. Her tan is monumental. She spent all summer parked on a chaise by our pool, barking out orders and slathering on Coppertone 8. Her skin is a stark brown contrast to the clean white of her gown. Roger waits for her at the altar in his dark tux and starched white shirt, his hair at attention, eyes misty. The music soars up to the painted ceiling, swelling to fill the room. The notes are loud and clear, resonating in my head. This is not what I want.

The reception is a triumph of fresh flowers and tiny fairy lights. A faux antique crystal chandelier hangs from the peak of the ballroom ceiling, and small crystal lamps sit on each table, casting dappled light over the warm wooden dance floor and the groups of guests happily chatting away.

An assortment of silk neckties and black bow ties hangs from the backs of the damask-covered chairs as everyone loosens up, enjoying themselves and the fully stocked bar set up under a sparkling arbor just outside on the patio. The photographer is making his rounds. Everyone and everything are fair game for a candid shot, including the cake table and the eight layers of spun sugar and fondant he is casing as he clicks by.

I am ducking and dashing my way through the crowd of long-lost grade school friends and random guys who sold my dad his first boat or whatever. My head is down, and I'm trying not to rub up against anyone too old or too friendly as I navigate my way away from the head table, toward the square of indigo sky calling to me from the wall of open patio doors.

I am making a sincere attempt to ditch Shane, my grabby dinner partner, along the way. My progress is slow because it seems that every two or three steps I have to stop when someone taps me on the shoulder or reaches for my hand with a smile and says, "It will be your turn soon," or, "You must be so proud of your sister today," or, my personal favorite, "Oh, Leah, sorry, I thought you were your sister."

Once outside I stop to rest. I breathe a sigh of relief, leaning up against the side of the building, the brickwork catching my curled hair. I have been clutching my pink bouquet so tight up against my chest, using it almost like a shield, that when I let down my guard and release it slowly, crushed rose petals shower my feet. The party hums behind me.

"Don't you tire of the constant comparisons?" a female voice asks as I twitch a couple of pink petals from the tops of my toes.

I force myself to smile before I look up, but it's not a meddling relative or even a friend of my mother's who gets all her gossip about our family secondhand at the local beauty parlor during a weekly shampoo set. It's Valerie. I swallow the polite argument I had ready and give her a smile. My resentment's been rendered unnecessary.

She's wearing a navy blue and white dotted swiss dress with puffed cap sleeves, a big bow at the neck, and a huge, floppy white hat, the kind of hat that only British women can get away with at British weddings. She's obviously confused a simple summer wedding for a day at the races, but she seems to be loving it.

She steps toward me, wobbling a little in her

snappy spectators. Her eyes scan the revelers inside the room. She stops, rolls back the front brim of her hat with her hand for a better view of my face, and announces, skeptically, "Frankly, I don't see it."

Knowing Valerie, I'm sure there was a chart or a graph or some other scientific research involved before she made this pronouncement, but I am wondering if she can honestly see anything past that hat. It's monstrous.

I follow her gaze and look across the flushed faces swarming the bar, the three bartenders in pink vests chipping ice and mixing drinks as fast as they can. I look past the tables circled with guests just finishing up their prime rib and new potatoes to my sisters huddled together near the head table, cloistered from the rest of the world by an elevated platform draped in satin and their superior attitude.

It's weird, but when I was inside the party, at the table with my sisters, in the mix, all warm and jostled, they looked rosy and smiling and benevolent to me. Now, from out here, they look taut and shiny and tense. And maybe even a little bit scared.

"Sometimes," I say, sighing as I reach up to flip the brim of her hat back down, "neither do I."

Valerie nods and disappears onto the dance floor. I watch her for a beat and then take the small step up onto the parquet floor, too, losing myself in the cloud of muggy air and meaty breath of tipsy forty-year-olds.

Everyone seems to be moving toward the bar while I sputter and struggle to make it toward the head table at the opposite end of the room. I climb onto the platform, lifting the back of my hem to clear the steps. A few ragged staples that started out the day cleverly tucked and hidden away in the swagged pink fabric have sprung loose, leaving the left side looking saggy and crooked.

I flop into my seat, glad to see my sisters have moved on and that Shane and the other wedding boys are presently pounding a bottle of champagne at a table in the corner.

I drop my bouquet between an engraved place card and an empty wineglass. Petals drift as I shove the dirty plates and stained napkins out of my way to make room for my elbows.

The band is ratcheting it up since dinner is officially over. An old gray-haired guy, I think it's Roger's grandfather if I remember correctly from the receiving line, leans toward his companions, all gray-haired, too, and cups his hand around his ear in an attempt to hear over the music.

The hired event staff is scrambling. Pink vests are everywhere, dirty dishes disappearing like clockwork as the busboys clear the tables near the center of the room and lift off the round tops and roll them away, spinning them out through a door conveniently hidden in one of the side walls to make more room on the dance floor.

I search the cluttered table for a half glass of champagne or at least one with a little something left in it.

Freddie is off to France at the end of the month, and Yorke leaves tonight, as soon as the reception starts to wane and my mother deems it acceptable for her and Roger to slip away. A sleek black Town Car, with pink and white streamers trailing from the back and JUST MARRIED painted on the rear window, is parked in front of the reception hall, ready and waiting to whisk her off on her honeymoon.

Maybe I am going to miss them. Maybe I have been resenting them all summer because it is easier than letting them go. Maybe Valerie is right.

I drain the champagne from the bottom of someone's glass, hoping to drown all my thoughts or at least slam them deeper into the back of my head. I wince when the warm, flat liquid hits my tongue. Ugh, backwash. I hope it's not Roger's.

I set the glass down with a shudder and watch my sisters working the crowd. Handshakes and generous hugs, congratulations and *bonnes chances*, stop them at every table they pass.

Pride rushes through me, flushing my cheeks faster than the champagne, as Yorke moves through the room, brazen and unabashed. The long beaded train of her wedding dress is forgotten in her excitement and leaves a sweeping trail of destruction in her wake.

Delighted to be the center of attention, as always, tonight Yorke is the ultimate bride, elated to be here, surrounded by her family and adoring friends, happy to be exactly what she is, even if that does turn out to be just a louder, more exaggerated modern-day version of my mother.

Five feet away Freddie is almost flying under the radar, a mirror image of Yorke, sliding through the crowd with a shy smile, quietly finding her way without disruption or disgrace, unassuming and effortless, as always, thanking everyone as the well-wishes for her pour in from every side.

And me? I guess I am somewhere in between. Not quite Freddie, but not quite Yorke either. I don't know who I am, but I know who I am not. I am not just the pink one or the third one in line.

I have always been fighting the fact that we are so alike, but it's true—me and Yorke and Freddie, we are similar. You just have to look really closely to see our differences. I get it now.

Outside, the sun has set for sure, swallowed whole by a black sky dotted with stars, and the patio is swirling with loads of really drunk people. I slip through them, looking for a place to rest, to throw off my killer sandals and recover from a very intense bout of dancing on the slick wooden dance floor and Shane and his sweaty brow and grinding hips.

Passing by the tables that have been dragged just far enough away from the thumping upright bass, I slide easily past my older aunts and uncles and their handshakes and hugs and reminders that "Soon it will be your turn" with a smile because I know it's not true. They can think what they want.

Holding tight to a rose-filled arbor, I bend over and pull my sandals off one at a time. I stand and stretch, toes at the edge of the patio, the lawn sloping away on all sides, deep and lush.

Shane walks up behind me, suddenly and unevenly, his cheeks hot and pink, the top few buttons of his tuxedo shirt undone and the white sleeves rolled up to let his thick forearms at the air. He wraps his hand on top of mine.

"What was that last night, Leah?" he asks, his voice thick and boozy.

He looks into my eyes, kind of sad and penitent

and I realize I have been running from him all night, all summer really, and it is pointless, and I am tired. He is only going to follow. And that's not his fault.

I haven't made a choice. Ever. I've always waited for someone to make it for me—Shane, Yorke, Freddie, my mother, even Duffy. It's finally my turn, ready or not.

I grip my fingers under his hand and brace myself for the good-bye 'cause I am scared of giving up all the things I will have to give up if I give up Shane. My whole senior year, my whole life, everything will be different, and I am worried that I won't be brave enough.

And there's nothing wrong with Shane. He's nice. He's fit. He's supercute. He smells good. Occasionally he's funny. I've got it good. I get that. But my whole life has been about going along, living with what has been given to me, which is kind of hard to bitch about, because I've been given a lot, but that doesn't mean I have to drive around for the rest of my life with his hand weighing down my leg, does it?

"That was me breaking up with you," I say, low and solid.

"But," Shane says, looking a little stunned and a lot drunk, "but what about . . . " He stumbles.

I pull away, cutting him off from what I know he is going to say, what we both expected to be the logical sequence of events. Semesters full of Friday nights lost in his backseat, homecoming court, followed by prom and parties and graduation.

I grab my shoes and step away from him, trying to keep it together. My mother does not like a scene, and Shane's never done anything wrong, other than fit her mold.

"I'm sorry, Shane," I say, my voice as tight and dry as it is sure, "so sorry, but you're on your own." He stumbles, one step away from me, and releases my hand. I drop my shoes onto the patio and walk away.

I pass the little boys in striped clip-on ties and short-sleeved dress shirts dancing with little girls with flowers in their hair, and Yorke looking heavy, carrying the only secret she's ever been able to keep, the one that seals her fate, and Freddie, dancing cheek to cheek with Evan, tight and content in the middle of the dance floor, unwilling to give him up. And my mother, arms around my dad, wrapped safe and secure in her snug little world of family and friends. I do not feel left out or left behind. I feel free.

I pass the big white floppy hat and the friend that Valerie has become with a smile. No doubt she will pass on what she has witnessed here tonight. Soon enough Duffy will know everything.

I catch her eye and wave before I disappear, down a flight of stone steps and out into the night. I walk across the lawn. My footprints shine behind me in the moonlight on the thick, wet grass. I am finding my own way.

Seventeen

The first day of school is blooming hard and hot outside my classroom window, and it still feels like summer to me.

The days have been muggy and long. Life has moved in slow motion. The only thing that seems to be moving at all is my heart. It races, tight in my chest. I am counting down to I don't know what.

My mother's unhappiness with me is apparent. The slash of coral on her lips is cracked and stretched thin. She doesn't understand how I could let Shane go, or why. She worries what everyone will think.

She doesn't understand that I don't have to live her life, or Yorke's or Freddie's, to get everything I want. She wants to keep me tethered tight, because my sisters are gone and she has no one else left. Our house is very clean.

The final bell is still ringing, and I am out, crossing the street on my way to the parking lot, filling my lungs with fresh air and searching for my keys, which always seem to sink helplessly to the bottom of my bag.

I look up, and my eyes glue onto him. My feet trip over themselves on the hot, cracked pavement. A threadbare T-shirt stretches across his chest. I read it, my eyes flicking up to catch his. CAMP KEWAUNEE.

"So, is that where you've been?" I ask.

His smile cracks open, and I know, right then, that my heart has been racing for a reason.

My final few steps toward him are taller and straighter, evolution in practice, before I light to a landing just a breath away.

The toes of his scuffed work boots point toward

the sky as he leans up against the car. He slides his hands down his long legs. Then he looks up at me.

"I heard," he says.

"What did you hear?" I ask, stretching out next to him, the hot car instantly warming the backs of my legs.

"Just a story." He shrugs.

"Yeah?"

"A story of a girl," he says with a smirk and a smile. "She's blond, she's got these sisters . . ."

"Well." I stop him. "I am not that girl. This is not that story."

"I know," he says, nodding across the parking lot. Valerie is there, watching us on the sly, doing a spazzy dance of joy between the parked cars in the back, getting ready to add Cupid to the extracurriculars on her college applications.

"How does it end?" I ask, looking over at him.

He moves, his jeans sliding down a bit on his lean frame, the muscles in his back flexing as he turns toward the car and pulls open the passenger door.

He slides into a handsomely restored gunmetal

gray '69 Camaro with creamy white leather interior. The chrome shines, the polished paint reflects the open sky rolling over our heads, and the red-and-white plates read PORTER. It's perfect.

"Climb in," he says, "let's find out."

I eye him, and the car, suspiciously. He watches me, waiting quietly, his green eyes dancing.

"Yes," he finally admits, running his hands through his tangle of thick dark hair sheepishly, "it's mine."

His smile opens up wide, and I melt right there into a pool of solder, shimmering onto the street. I climb in, drop it into first, slide my hand into his, and put my foot to the floor. Watch for the sparks.